HE CAN'T REMEMBER, SHE CAN'T FORGET

HE CAN'T REMEMBER, SHE CAN'T FORGET

Linda S. Hoffman

This book was printed in the United States of America.

To order additional copies of this book, contact:
Xlibris Corporation
1-888-795-4274
www.Xlibris.com
Orders@Xlibris.com
20755

CONTENTS

To my mother Helen:
You are the foundation our family is built on.

To my late father Frank:
I miss you Daddy.

To my brothers Ray and Bobby:
I'm so proud of you both.

To my daughter Angela and Aimee:
Thank you for my grandchildren, I love you both very much.

To my mother in-law Dorothy and my father-in-law Jim:
I will always take care of your son.

ACKNOWLEDGMENTS

First and foremost I would like to express my deep love and gratitude to my brother and sister in-law Ray and Kathy Vilage. Without their financial and emotional support, this book would not have gone to press.

My deep appreciation to Adena who, after reading my rough draft believed in the power of my story enough to force me to complete my work.

There are not enough words to express my gratitude to my editor and cover designer Melissa Voit. The time we have spent together, molding this novel into the book you read today is priceless.

My love and thanks to Mrs. Krishna Sharma CEO of Sherman International Corporation. Our relationship has changed from employee to dear friends.

And finally to the special people in my life Bev, Margie, Joseph, Susie, Johti, Adrienne, Lolly, Michelle, The Carnegie Library of Munhall Fundraising Committee, and the staff at Michaels in West Mifflin. I am a better person today, because of your support.

PROLOGUE

Five years ago, my husband had a stroke; five years ago, my life changed forever. The day he had the stroke was the day I died. It sounds so dramatic, his stroke, I died, but in order to understand that statement, you'll have to read and then re-read this book.

It has taken me four years to put this story down on paper. I spent the first year crying everyday. Oh, I would be all right for about an hour or so, then the flood of despair would wash over me like a tidal wave. It would pound me down with such force that I thought I would drown in my own tears. Then it would pass and I would start to function again until the next wave of despair would come.

The stroke was bad enough, but the circumstances leading up to it and engulfing it is what cut the life out of me. I am not the same person that I used to be. I lost my drive to succeed, my desire to look to the future, my desire to feel.

He is not the same person he used to be. He has lost all memory of the events that happened.

He laughs, loves his grandchildren, loves his children, and enjoys life. He would have never been a part of their lives. He was too self-centered and self-serving to love or take care of anyone but himself.

That is my problem, there can be no closure. To fight and confront someone that has no memory of the person he was or the events that took place seems cruel. He has no knowledge of the hurt or pain he has caused.

All I can do is try and close the doors of my mind. One by one, each is a door to a bad memory. That is the only way I can survive.

I hate the man that caused all the pain in my heart and life. I feel sorry for the man I live with today. After you read this novel, you will understand the title "HE CAN'T REMEMBER, SHE CAN'T FORGET."

CHAPTER ONE

The Beginning

It was a slow night in the emergency room at County General Hospital. Brad leaned up against the admissions desk and gazed down the dimly lit hallway. In the distance, he could see Marnie as she walked towards him. Her sultry moves sent currents of electricity up and down his spine. Marnie was the best thing that had happened to him in a long time, but also the most dangerous. Marnie brought emotions out in him that he had not felt in years. It sounded perfect, except for one thing; he was married. He did not plan to fall in love, it just happened. Marnie came along at a time in Brad's life when he needed excitement, danger, and lust. She filled his body with a passion that had long been buried.

As Marnie reached the desk, she brushed up against Brad. The feeling of her body took his breath away. *How can someone feel so wonderful without feeling any guilt? Probably,* he thought, *because his love for Carly, his wife, had died a long time ago.*

Marnie leaned over and whispered into Brad's ear, "If you like the feeling of my body with clothes on, then you'll love it without." She motioned for Brad to follow her down the hall. "Brad," she said loudly, "I need to discuss the status of Mr. Benson in room 227, could you come with me, please?" She walked with Brad down the hall and leaned in close to him. "Are you going to meet me tonight?"

"Of course I am, and if you brush up against me one more time, I'll drag you into an empty room and make love to you right there." Brad's smile revealed his thoughts to her. "You check into our usual place, and I'll join you at the end of my shift." They had been meeting at a secluded motel hidden behind a row of tall pine trees, down in a deep valley; out of view from prying eyes.

Brad finished his shift, punched out, and went to the locker room to take a shower. The hot water set the mood for what was to come. Marnie checked into the room and anxiously waited for Brad to end his shift and meet her there. The past two years had not been good for Marnie. Her marriage had ended, she had moved to a new town, and she had been very lonely, until Brad. No one had ever made her feel the way Brad did. His experience, his gentleness, his passion, made her want him more. Plus, he was so excited by her youth that it brought out the best in him. Her firm body and energetic love making was exactly what Brad needed, and Marnie aimed to please.

Brad knocked on the door to the motel room. Marnie's heart skipped a beat. As she opened the door, a heat rushed over her entire body. She fell straight into Brad's arms and their night of passionate lovemaking began. After they had consumed each other completely, they laid in each others arms, totally exhausted. "Ok, stud man, when can we do this again?"

"Come on Marnie, you know we have to be careful. If Carly finds out, I'm dead meat at home and at work."

"Oh, you worry too much. How's she going to find out? She's never home, and when she is you two don't talk anyway."

"Yes, but she's not stupid and some day she'll figure out that I'm not working overtime as much as I say I am. Thank God, she doesn't ever see my pay. Then for sure, she'd know. Don't forget Carly's going out of town on business in two weeks. She'll be gone for eleven whole days. Just think, I can spend all my free time with you without worrying."

"Oh Brad," Marnie whispered, "If only we could be together forever, that would make my life complete. I love you so much."

"Be patient Marnie, I have to take things one day at a time. We'll be together soon, just be patient."

Over the past few months, Carly had become a source of money to Brad. She gave him half her pay towards the bills, but it wasn't enough. The credit cards had been maxed out, and money had become tight. Pay a card, get a new card; a vicious cycle that would end up choking him one day. Thank God, he got the mail every day. If Carly would get the charge receipts and saw the motel charges, he'd be dead. Somewhere along the way, he had stopped feeling anything for Carly. It had happened so long ago, that he could no longer remember the last time that he had felt any emotion of love towards her.

*　　*　　*

Brad Stevenson and Carly Abbott met in the mid '60's when they were both fifteen years old. Their lives could not have been more different. Carly came from a "Beaver Cleaver" household.

John and Mary Abbott, Carly's parents, loved one another and their children very much. John worked hard in the Steel Mill and Mary stayed at home. Life in the Abbott household consisted of rules, regulations, and structure. They had a set dinnertime, bedtime, chores, and church. They gave each other a kiss good morning and a kiss good night. Not because you had to, but because you wanted to. They were not wealthy by standards of money, but wealthy by the love in their family. John worked hard so that Carly and her brother Tom did not have to go to public school. The Steel town schools were tough. Everyone that went there was destined to work in the mill. Although John made a good living in the mill, he wanted more for Carly and Tom. Carly, however, liked the wild boys, ones more dangerous then the catholic school guys. She wanted excitement and she found more then she bargained for; she found Brad.

CHAPTER TWO

Jack Stevenson

Brad's father, Jack Stevenson was born in Saundersville, a coal-mining town in Ohio. Jack's parents Sylvia and Charles had four children, two boys and two girls. Until Jack was older, he did not realize how poor their family really was. Every minute of every day, Charles worked hard just to try to make ends meet. The mine was a cruel place to work. It was dark, cold, and damp, day in and day out. The chill in his bones didn't leave until it was time to go back into the hellhole again. Sylvia struggled to take care of Charles and four children. No luxury items in their home, just hard work. Sylvia cooked, cleaned, and washed clothes by hand and hung them on the line to dry. Not an easy life, but Sylvia loved Charles and her babies, so she never complained.

You tend to grow old before your time in the mines. You have trouble breathing, walking, and the cold makes your bones ache. Jack hated to watch his father work so hard for so little money. No matter what, he wasn't going to end up working in the mines. The one pleasure in Jack's life was reading the magazines and books about travel in the school library. Hong Kong, France, Italy, he wanted to travel to all of them. His life wasn't going to be working in a hole in the ground of Saundersville.

When Jack was twelve, his beloved grandfather Bradley Stevenson died of black lung disease. When Jack was seventeen, his father died of the same disease. From that day on, Jack had no doubt in his mind that he would never step one foot in the mines, not ever.

Jack was the oldest at seventeen, Janet was fifteen, Margaret was thirteen, and Skip was eleven. Being the oldest, the family responsibilities were falling onto Jack's shoulders. He loved his family very much and held his mother in the highest respect, but he couldn't; he vowed he wouldn't, be stuck in Saundersville forever.

After school, Jack worked odd jobs to help Sylvia with the food money. He kept a small amount for himself; if the time ever came when he could get out of town, he wanted to be ready. Thank God, Charles had saved some money in the bank. It wasn't much, but Sylvia needed all the help she could get. She took in laundry and sewing, and did house keeping and cleaning at night. The girls helped with the laundry and sewing and Skip went with her to clean. Everyone worked hard to survive. It was hard, but love held them together.

The news from overseas wasn't good at that time. WWII was escalating and Jack was going to be drafted. The last place, next to Saundersville, he wanted to go was in the Army, so he enlisted in the Navy. He hoped the Navy would open the world to him, and he wouldn't be disappointed. The news that Jack had to go into the service hit Sylvia hard. Having just lost Charles and now Jack leaving was almost too much to bear. Janet, Margaret, and Skip all cried at the news. Jack had become the only father figure in their life, even though he was only seventeen years old.

Days went by quickly and it was time for Jack to leave. The whole family went to the bus station to see him off. Sylvia took Jack's face in her hands and looked in his eyes. "Son, you're not a boy anymore, you're a man. If Dad were here, he'd be so proud of you. You go and serve your country, and see the world and don't worry about anything. This is your chance to get away from the mines. Just keep safe and come home to us," she told her son as tears were streaming down her cheeks. She knew Jack would never come back to Saundersville. If she had the chance, she would leave too.

As Jack boarded the bus, he looked back at his family, and his town. He prayed to God that if he made it through the war, the only time he would have to come back would be to visit, not to stay. Jack left with mixed emotions. He was very worried how his family would survive without him. His mother was still reeling from the death of his father and the kids would miss him. Even at his age, he felt he should be the one to have carried the burdens, not his mother. Yet, the call away from the mines and Saundersville gave Jack the possibility to create a new life for himself, the chance for his dreams to become a clear reality. If he didn't leave then, he would have never left. As much as it hurt, he had no regrets about leaving Saundersville. The only thing the Navy was to Jack was a ticket around the world. He performed his duties well, but when it came to shore leave, he was eager. If only shore leave was as long as the time at sea, but with the war raging around him, he was lucky to see any towns at all. France and Italy were both so exquisite that it took his breath away. Even in the midst of conflict, he could see the beauty in both places. Every stop fed his soul with the food it needed to survive. It gave him the strength to know he'd never go back to his old life.

What he would do after his tour of duty he did not know. His hitch would soon be over and he needed a plan for when he got back to the states. The beauty of the countries he had visited was etched in his brain. The museums and the elaborately decorated hotels were more magnificent than he could have ever imagined. Walking through the lobbies and seeing the care and detail that was put into every aspect of the operation inspired Jack. He decided that his career would center on hotel operations. He would go to school and one day own and operate his own hotel.

With his separation money and VA loan, he searched for a hotel management school. He found the school he wanted in Northridge, Pennsylvania. He got a job as a short order cook at night so that he could go to school in the day. When school break came, he would change his night shift to the day turn. What he did not know was that this shift would change his life and the lives of others.

CHAPTER THREE

Denise Jenkins

Denise Jenkins was quite a beauty. She had long flowing black hair, eyes the color of black marbles, and a figure sent down from heaven above. Still in high school, she looked as though she was much older then her age of seventeen. She was very active in school, theater mainly. She longed to go to New York or Hollywood to become a star. God knows she had the looks and the talent. Yet at seventeen, they were only dreams, but someday, they might come true. After all, she was acting in school plays and reading about New York. So when the time came, she planned to be ready. She never counted on meeting Jack Stevenson.

It was a hot summer day when Denise Jenkins strolled into the Corner Diner. Her long black hair fell softly upon her delicate shoulders. The soft floral print sundress she wore hugged her curves in an inviting way. Heads turned whenever she walked into a room. When she entered the diner, one head in particular turned and spun. That was Jack's. He had traveled around the world, but never had seen anyone as beautiful as Denise. From the first look, she stole his heart away. The age difference should have been an issue, but it wasn't. Denise was seventeen, and Jack was a very worldly twenty-two.

It became a whirlwind affair. Two people feeding off each other's needs. Denise wanted to get out of Northridge and go to New York. Jack wanted someone to love and be by his side to pursue his dreams. Too bad that their attraction was so strong and they weren't more careful. After a small wedding, Denise soon after found out that she was pregnant. The thought of having a baby terrified her. She was only eighteen, a baby herself, and what about her life? What about her dreams of New York? If only she had been more careful. Jack wasn't exactly thrilled either. Having a wife was one thing, but throw in a baby, and that messes up all the plans!

Well, nothing was going to stop him. Denise would just have to take care of the baby when it came. After all, she was the woman and she should have been more careful. Denise, as pregnant as ever, really resented Jack's ability to continue his pursuits. She really loved Jack and the thought of having his child. Yet she wanted her dreams as well.

Denise and Jack had the most beautiful baby boy. They named their little boy Brad after Jack's grandfather Bradley. Under the circumstances Jack, Denise, and Brad were a happy family. After graduating hotel school, Jack worked two jobs to make ends meet. Denise stayed home and took care of Brad. Six years go by, with the same routine day in and day out and by that time, Jack became restless. He had gotten to the point where he couldn't spin his wheels in Northridge any longer. Jack received an offer to manage a motel in Chicago with a chance of getting his own hotel eventually. He took the offer, yet Denise just could not go with him. It was too late for her. Brad was in school, and her father was ill. She was afraid to go with Jack. Jack loved Denise and Brad, yet if he would not have gone then, he would have never gone. He begged for Denise to go with him, but she just couldn't. At the age of twenty-eight, Jack packed his bags, got on a bus, and left. He couldn't die in Northridge, he hoped that she would follow; yet she never did.

When Jack left, Brad was crushed. Jack was Brad's hero. Brad blamed himself that Jack left. As a little boy, he cried, as a younger man, he rebelled. Denise tried to be a good mother. Deep in her soul, she wished that she would have gone with Jack, but it was too late. She'd never be able to turn back the clock now.

Denise worked nights at the diner where she first met Jack. Denise's mother watched Brad at night and she slept while he was at school. The problem came in the summer when school was out. She had a hard time keeping him out of trouble. Nonetheless, she had to work. What little money Jack sent just was not enough. They barely made it with her job and his money. The years took their toll. Brad was twelve and Denise was thirty going on a hundred. She was tired, lonely, and frustrated. Work, sleep, Brad, that's all she had in life. Thank God, she was a damn good waitress. Her tips kept her going. She was still beautiful at thirty and had a good personality. Moreover, she was a shameless flirt; innocent but shameless. Hey, if it meant good tips, what's the harm?

Then, one night about two a.m., in walked Sam Tillton. Six feet of the most gorgeous masculinity you'd ever want to meet. He was a blue eyed, blonde haired factory worker. He took her breath away. No one after Jack had ever done that to her and it scared her to death. Sam was a charmer, always on the prowl. Her wit and his sense of humor made them a fun couple. On the weekends when she didn't work, they danced the nights away. It felt so good to laugh. It was something she had not allowed herself to do for years. There was only one problem, Brad. Sam didn't want a child to interrupt his life. He was a forty-five year old man who wanted only to have fun, not the responsibility of someone else's child.

When Brad turned thirteen, it should have been a big day for him. Yet it wasn't. Denise and Sam announced that they were getting married. Brad didn't like Sam; likewise, Sam didn't like Brad. Brad didn't want to move, change schools, or leave his friends, besides nobody would ever take his father Jack's place. After a lot of arguing, they finally came to a decision. Brad would stay at grandmas and finish school with his friends. Sam was thrilled, Brad was thrilled, but Denise was crushed. She had hoped that Sam and Brad would eventually get along, but that would never happen. Sam wanted his own children, and although he didn't like Brad, he just felt that it was Jack's responsibility to take care of his son. Brad was determined that Jack would come for him. Yet, Jack never came, never called, and Sam and Brad never got along.

Denise had always wanted a little girl and what a beauty she was. Denise's black hair and Sam's big blue eyes. She took even

Brad aback. After fifteen years of being an only child, it was kind of nice to have a little sister.

Denise wasted no time in adding to her family, and gave birth to a bouncing baby boy. Jerry was the picture of Sam, blonde hair and blue eyes. After holding his son, Sam couldn't understand how Jack was able to turn his back on Brad. His feelings began to soften towards Brad. For the first time, he understood how Brad must have been feeling; not having a father around to count on.

CHAPTER FOUR

Carly and Brad

When Carly and Brad first met, it was as if rockets went off in the sky. He was the troublemaker, and she was the one looking for adventure. It was an instant attraction. They started to date, much to the dismay of Carly's parents. They wanted Carly to marry a promising young man, not some rebel without a cause. Yet, they could not convince Carly to look around; she had found the man that she wanted. They dated for three years. Carly was thrilled but she didn't know that you couldn't change a hound dog. Even though Brad loved Carly, he just could not stop howling around behind her back. Maybe that was okay before you are married, but when would the howling stop?

Carly and Brad both graduated high school. After graduation, they were engaged. Brad wanted to join the Navy like his father Jack, but at the last minute, he joined the Air Force. The Vietnam War was raging at the time and they needed men to load the planes with supplies, so they stationed Brad in California in warehousing. The separation away from Carly distressed Brad. The prospect of both of them in California, however, made him smile. Brad, Carly, and sunny California, what a combination! Carly couldn't wait to marry Brad and start a family with him. John and Mary had finally felt that Brad had taken a turn for the better, in having joined the Air Force. Maybe, just maybe, they would be happy.

Brad came home on leave at Christmas after basic training. His visit with Carly wasn't long enough to suit either one of them. It was so hard to part knowing that they would not see each other until September for the wedding. Brad and Carly held each other as if they would never see each other again. As Brad boarded the plane, Carly's heart sank; she would miss him so much.

Brad sat on the plane, he felt a sudden chill go up his spine. *What the hell am I doing?* he thought to himself. *Here I am, off to California and I'm getting married! What a jerk I am. Sun, fun, women, and I've committed myself to a wedding. Well,* he thought, *if I only have nine months of bachelor-hood, let the games begin!*

Instead of planning for his own wedding, he started planning for a party. His first step was to get an apartment off base. Second, check out the chicks, and third make sure Carly never found out. Brad got settled on base, then found an apartment. He shared it with a couple of buddies until Carly arrived.

Denise wrote Brad that his Aunt Edna called to tell her that his father was in Fresno, California. She gave Brad the address and told him to go see his father. It had been years since Brad had seen or even talked to Jack. He was tentatively excited to go see him. He didn't call Jack to say that he was coming. Maybe he was afraid that Jack wouldn't want to see him. He bought a bus ticket and took a chance.

*　　*　　*

Jack owned a hotel in Fresno called the Gold Coast. What a shock it was when Brad's cab pulled up to the front of the hotel. He was truly impressed. Brad went in and asked the desk clerk to page Jack Stevenson. The desk clerk asked, "And who can I say wants to see him?"

Brad told the man, "His son." Jack and Brad met face to face for the first time in years. There was no denying that Brad was Jack's son, the resemblance was uncanny.

The meeting went well, but over the years, Jack had become suspicious of anyone he thought had an angle against him. *What did Brad really want?* he wondered. Brad made it clear to Jack that all he wanted was to see him after all these years and to get to know him as a father. He told Jack about Carly and their upcoming wedding. Jack canceled all of his appointments and booked two seats on the next plane to Vegas. Jack wanted to show off in front of Brad. From partying to showgirls, they did it all! After his meeting with Jack, Brad was regretting the thought of getting married, but it was too late now.

Jack had prior commitments and couldn't make it home for Brad and Carly's wedding. He sent a generous check and card wishing them both the best of luck. He knew that he would get to spend time with them when they both came back to California. Brad boarded the plane home with mixed emotions. He really did love Carly, but the thought of responsibility and commitment terrified him. He liked to party and he liked to run, neither one fit into the marriage plans.

CHAPTER FIVE

Their Life Together Begins

September 17th was absolutely gorgeous, the perfect day for a wedding. Carly looked stunning and Brad looked handsome, a typical bride and groom. John, Mary, and Denise were all keeping their fingers crossed that this marriage would work. Denise knew Brad and she hoped that Carly could settle him down. Carly was the best thing that ever happened to Brad and Denise wanted it to stay that way. John, more than Mary, had his fear for his daughter. He'd been around the block and knew what Brad was made of. He prayed that Brad would not hurt his daughter. Nothing in life was certain and he just hoped for the best for her.

The plane ride to sunny California was full of excitement and wonder. Carly had never been away from Northridge and this was not a short trip. You couldn't just run home if something went wrong. Brad, on the other hand, was very nervous. Responsibility, that scary word, was something that he was not used to assuming. Another person depended on him for everything. Hell, he had a hard enough time taking care of himself, let alone someone else.

All remnants of Brad's bachelor life were cleaned out of the apartment. God forbid, Carly would ever suspect what had been going on there. She would jump back on a plane and head straight for home. Brad thought to himself, *I have to make this work, if only for Carly's sake.*

The first three years went actually quite well. Carly fell right in with Brad's life style. They had great fun together, day and night. Jack fell in love with Carly the minute he met her. Having not been a father to Brad for all those years, he wanted to make sure he was there for him now. Whatever Carly and Brad needed he tried to give it to them. They never asked for anything, so Jack would send money and presents regularly. Carly was glad to have at least some part of a family there. She missed her father, mother, and her brother Tom very much. Carly was a good wife. She worked in a small gift shop off base to keep busy. She did all the normal wifely duties and loved every minute of it. Yet something was missing. She wanted to have a baby.

The idea of a baby didn't sit well with Brad at all. He liked the life he had with Carly; it was better then he thought it would be. Besides a transfer could come down at any time to go to Vietnam. A baby was the last thing on his mind. He had never thought of having children; he just wasn't the fatherly type. It was that responsibility word again. Who needed more of that? But, nature and Carly's determination dealt Brad a hand he wasn't prepared to play. Carly had become pregnant and was positively thrilled; yet Brad couldn't have been anymore unhappy at the idea of a child.

The news of her pregnancy flipped his whole world upside down. He didn't hide his feelings from her at all. What should have been a happy occasion for Carly turned into pure misery! She did not let anyone know how unhappy with Brad's reaction she really was. Jack was elated about the news of a grandchild. Maybe he could be a better grandfather then he had been a father. John, Mary, and Denise were a nervous wreck. If only they were both home. Brad still had seven months to go in the Air Force, and Carly did not want to come home without him. Between the stress of her pregnancy and dealing with Brad's disinterest, Carly was having a tough time. Brad was sinking deeper and deeper into his old ways. Like a spoiled child, he was acting up all over again and it was breaking Carly's heart. With one more month of pregnancy to go, Carly faced moving to Fresno to have the baby. Brad was discharged from the Air Force and Jack had offered him a job at his hotel, plus a place to live. So they packed up and traveled five hundred miles to Fresno. Jack was unaware of Brad's true feelings about the baby. Carly hadn't told anyone about their problems, but soon Jack would see for himself.

Carly's labor was intense. The baby was breech and both mother and daughter had problems. To get the baby out required surgery and Carly was terrified. Her beautiful little girl may die and Brad could have cared less. All he was doing was working and drinking. She had to beg him to be with her in the hospital, and even then, he couldn't wait to leave. It was touch and go for about two months, but her little girl Cassie was just fine. Running back and forth to the hospital exhausted Carly and with no help from Brad, she had had it. Jack had become aware of the problems that Brad and Carly were having, but tried to stay out of it. After all what right did he have to try to be a father now after all those years?

"A visit home to Northridge is just what the doctor ordered," Jack told Carly. "Denise wants to see you and the baby and so do your parents. Besides, you need to get away from here for a while to clear your head."

Carly started to cry, "How did you know Brad and I were having trouble?"

Jack hugged Carly and said, "It's pretty obvious that he's spending more time out and less time with you and Cassie. I can't tell him to stop, but maybe some time apart will give him time to get his act together." For Brad and Cassie's sake, Carly hoped that Jack was right. Brad was very happy that Carly and the baby were going back home for two weeks. What a break. Just when he had heard about a big blowout some friends were having in Hollywood. He could never have gone with Carly home, so now he was free. He called the guys and made plans, and anxiously waited for the time when Carly and the baby would leave.

Driving Carly and the baby to the airport, Brad's mind wandered as he thought about the fun that was to come after they left. Carly looked at Brad and said, "Are you happy that we won't be here for two weeks?"

"Of course not, I just have a lot on my mind," he said to Carly red-faced, as he was caught red-handed deep in alien thoughts.

"Well I'm sure that you've made plans for while I'm gone, please don't think that I'm that stupid."

Brad looked in her eyes and said, "See, there you go thinking the worst. You know dad's busy now; I'll be working my ass off while you're gone. Just go and see everyone and don't worry about anything here." With that statement, he kissed her and Cassie good-bye. He left the airport, anticipating two fun-filled weeks alone.

John and Mary were at the airport to pick up their daughter and granddaughter Cassie. I don't know who was happier, Carly to be home, or John and Mary to finally see their granddaughter for the first time. Carly did her best to hide her problems from her parents, but every time she tried to call Brad and got no answer, it showed on her face. Mary sat Carly down the day before she was to return to Fresno. "Carly it's none of my business, but are you and Brad having problems?"

Carly started to cry and all the emotions that she had held inside for so long finally came flooding out. "Oh Mom, ever since I got pregnant and had Cassie, Brad has become so cold and distant."

"Carly you know men have a difficult time with change, give him time, he'll come around, you'll see." Mary said the right words to her daughter, yet even she didn't believe them.

Carly was too sad for a simple adjustment period. She thought to herself, *If only mom is right. Maybe that's all he needs, a little more time and he will come around.* She still loved him so much and in her heart, she knew that he still loved her and he loved the baby. He just had a hard time adjusting to change; he was never good at that.

While Carly was in Northridge, Brad was in rare form. Work all day, party all night, just like the good old days. Jack watched all that and wondered when it was going to end. He planned not to say anything to Brad until Carly came home. Maybe he just needed to blow off some steam and would settle down once his wife and daughter came home. Carly and Cassie bid a heartfelt goodbye to everyone in Northridge and boarded the plane to

Fresno. Not sure of what she would find once she got there, she prayed that her life would be better than when she left; but that was not to be.

The look on Brad's face as she exited the plane told her that she was the last person he wanted to see. He looked exhausted and all played out. His disinterest in her trip home and the lack of affection towards her and Cassie made her realize that her place was at home in Northridge, not here. She gave time for Brad to warm up to her and Cassie, but that never happened. Her mother said to be patient, but after weeks of coldness and silence, enough was finally enough. If he wanted to act like a child, then he could do it without her and Cassie.

Jack was finally over keeping quiet about this whole mess. Maybe after two divorces himself, he felt that he had a right to at least try to give Brad some well-needed advice. Jack cornered Brad into the kitchen of the hotel and said, "Look son, maybe I have no right to speak up, but don't you think enough is enough? You have a beautiful wife and baby, why are you willing to mess it all up for a good time?"

Brad looked at his father and said, "Really Dad, don't you think that you should mind your own business? I mean seriously, I don't think you have any room to talk after two divorces and leaving my mother."

"I didn't leave your mother, she wouldn't come with me. I begged her to come with me. As for my two divorces, my experience tells me that you are on the same path; don't make the same mistakes I did."

Brad looked Jack in the eyes and said, "I think it's a little late for you to pull the father act on me, so butt out." With that statement, Jack sadly left Brad well enough alone.

Carly was having some health problems; nerves, stress, and depression had finally worn her out. She had made her decision that she had put off for weeks; it would be time for her and Cassie to go back home to Northridge for good, with or without Brad.

Carly told Jack of her plans and he was heartbroken. Carly and the baby were as close to a family as he had had in years. If only

Brad would have listened to him. The time had finally come to tell Brad that she and the baby were leaving to go back home for good.

"Brad, I want you to come home with me so we can try to be a family again. California and your so-called friends have taken you away from Cassie and me. We need you, and love you, your friends won't be there forever, but we will."

"Carly, how can I leave Jack at the height of his busy season, can't you wait until October? Maybe you'll change your mind by then. I really don't want to leave California." Brad was surprised by Carly's statement. He knew that she wasn't happy, but figured that she'd get over it.

"NO, Brad I'm not waiting! You've been cold and distant and I won't raise Cassie in this kind of atmosphere. You need to grow up and know that I love you and need you as a man, not a boy who wants to play."

"I'm not going to leave Dad stuck through his busy time. If you're hell bent on leaving now, then go. I'll leave in October and bring our things home with me." "Ok, he finally did it; he had pushed too hard. But maybe this could work; he'll have a lot more fun, then go home and try to be a dutiful husband. *Hell, Carly will be happy, she'll stay with John and Mary and they'll spoil Cassie like crazy. Carly will be too busy to worry about what I'm doing,* he thought to himself as he looked almost through Carly.

Carly saw the far away look in Brad's eyes, she knew that her leaving was not what he was thinking about, but about all the fun that he would have once they were gone until he was forced to finally join them in Northridge. "If you think you're going to come back to Northridge and pick up where you left off here, you've got another thing coming. If you can't come back and try to be a husband to me and a father to your daughter, then don't come back at all. I'd be better off alone than with a man who felt obligated to be with his family, rather then wanting to be with them."

Packing up to leave was the hardest thing that Carly ever had to do. She had no idea if Brad would ever join her in Northridge, or even if he still loved her. Yet she knew in her heart that she couldn't stay there like that, lonely and confused; at least at home, she could think without pressure from Brad.

Again, as Carly and Cassie boarded the plane, she was crying. "Brad, I'm never coming back here. If you really love Cassie and me, you'll join us in October. Remember; don't come home unless you truly, in your heart, want to." With that, she kissed Brad goodbye and didn't look back, she couldn't. She knew that she wouldn't have the strength to stop herself from running right back into his arms.

There weren't a lot of differences between Jack and Brad. The only big difference was that Jack knew how to make money and Brad knew how to blow it. From June to October, Jack and Brad argued regularly. Jack was no saint, but he could see what was happening and he didn't like it. Brad spent every free minute playing around. Sun, fun, women, and anything else that caught his fancy. He threw money around like he was rich, but he wasn't, and the bills started to pile up. Jack loved Carly and the baby and hated to see how Brad was acting. He was actually looking forward to Brad leaving in October, if he was leaving.

By the time September came, Brad had to make a decision, stay or go; Carly or California? Maybe it was time to leave, he was getting pretty close to getting in trouble and if that happened, he'd lose everything. Besides, he could settle down for a while, let the smoke clear, then see if any of the old gang was still around. Hey, fun is fun wherever you are. In October, he loaded his truck, told Jack goodbye, and headed home to Northridge. He probably never should have left California.

CHAPTER SIX

Home to Northridge

Brad had a lot of time to think driving back home to Northridge. Choices rummaged through his head; try to be a good husband and father, or have fun and the hell with everyone and everything. And what about a job? He couldn't count on Jack; with the way he left Fresno there was no chance in hell that Jack would help. Jack was now done with helping him. This time, he would have to show up for work on time and sober; no more daddy to count on. As far as a place to live, well, Brad was sure Carly had spilled her guts to John and Mary about how unhappy he had made her. Living with them was out of the question, for sure. There was so much to think about. It would have been easier just to stay in Fresno. Yet easy was a word that Brad didn't know.

Driving at night under the stars with the cool air flowing around him, he decided to give his marriage another try. Hey, it's not like he didn't love Carly and Cassie; he just liked his freedom and not having to answer to anyone. When Carly and Brad were first married, they shared a passion for love and life together. He started to remember the way that Carly used to look at him. She had a way about her that made him go crazy. All she had to do was look at him a certain way and he wanted to make love to her wherever they were. Brad would hold her so tight that he felt their hearts beat as one. He remembered one time pulling over on the side of the freeway and making love to Carly under the exit sign, another time in the middle of the desert on the way to Las Vegas. Those memories were just some of the many that made him laugh aloud.

What the hell's wrong with me? he asked himself. *Why can't I quit running and searching? What the hell am I looking for?* It was more like, what was he running from? Maybe he was running away from bad memories, or maybe the idea of responsibility. Whatever it was, it was time that he made a change and settled down, for everyone's sake.

*   *   *

The thought of seeing Brad after all these months frightened Carly. The only thing that kept her going was the memories of what she and Brad shared earlier in their marriage. All she ever wanted to do was give Brad the love and stability that she knew he longed for. She prayed that being back in Northridge together with their family around for support, their relationship would finally get back the passion and love that they once had. She was committed again to give Brad love and understanding; in return, she hoped to get her husband back and to establish a relationship between Brad and Cassie. She took a deep breath, looked out the window, and waited for her future to pull into the driveway.

*   *   *

Driving into Northridge, Brad felt somewhat certain that his change of heart and new determination would re-ignite his passion and love for Carly, and make him into the father Cassie needed. Brad took a deep breath and slowly pulled into John and Mary's driveway; the driveway that would lead to his new life, he hoped. Brad looked up to see Carly run down the driveway. Her eyes were bright with excitement; her skin glowed in the early fall air. *God she's beautiful,* he thinks to himself. He really had forgotten how one look from her could make him feel. He got out of the truck and swept Carly up in his arms. He held her so tight he could feel her heart beat, and kissed her with such intensity that even surprised him.

Brad held her face in his hands and looked deep into her dark brown eyes. He said, "Carly, I've been a real asshole, and I'm sure you're not going to argue with me about that, but honey, I really want to make up for all the bad and hurtful things I've done to you and Cassie. You deserve a husband and Cassie needs a full-time father. I do love both of you and if you can forgive me, I'm going to try very hard not to let you down again."

Carly melted into Brad's arms. She had waited so long to hear Brad say those words that she could hardly believe her ears. "Brad, I have no idea what made you so determined to put our life back together again, and frankly, I don't care. All I know is that I've always loved you and I always will. And if you and I both try, Cassie will grow up in a happy and loving family." Carly's heart was overjoyed and her soul was filled with a new energy.

Brad looked around and said, "Hey, where's my girl, it's been months since I've seen her. Get Cassie out here." He looked up to see John walking her down the yard. "Oh, my God, she's walking!" It had been five months since Brad had seen Cassie, and he was worried that she wouldn't remember him. But Cassie surprised him and put her arms right up to him. He held her close and whispered in her little ear, "Daddy's home now and I promise never to leave you or mommy again."

John and Mary rented an apartment for Brad and Carly. John had hoped that Brad would have stayed in Fresno, as far away from Carly and Cassie as possible, but that didn't happen. So the next best thing was to set them up in their own place and have as little contact with Brad as possible. "Once a runner, always a runner," he told Mary. "Those kind of guys can't change, it's in their blood." Mary, on the other hand, wanted the marriage to work. Cassie needed a father and a stable home to live in. She prayed that in time, Brad and Carly would strive together to give her that home. John only signed a six-month lease. He figured that was enough time to see if the marriage would work. After six months, they would be on their own. He didn't hold much hope that Brad would change; but only time would tell.

Carly felt her dreams were finally coming true. Brad was sweeter and kinder than ever. In her heart, she prayed that it would last. Brad was eager to get a job, but the mills in Northridge were laying off. He went to County General Hospital to apply for work in the kitchen, but the only opening was for an orderly. The fact that Brad was six feet tall, very strong and an ex-serviceman got him the job. The hospital felt an ex GI would be disciplined enough to be on time and perform his duties without question. Finally, the money was coming in, and the hospital provided health coverage for the whole family.

He took the job and started training the next day. After training, he was put on night turn. The last man hired always got the worst shift. The plus to the shift was that it paid $1.00 an hour more. The extra money would help. One baby in the household was ok, but no more. He actually liked things just the way they were. The apartment was fine for the first six months, but it was getting crowded with all of the baby's things. So a house was the next step in their life. Carly wanted a garden and Cassie needed a yard to play in. The responsibility of the house scared Brad just a little, but he wanted to make Carly happy, so the deed was signed.

For the next three years, life in the Stevenson household couldn't have been better. Carly planted her garden and Brad worked around the house. Even John had to admit that Brad had made a complete turn around. Their love was spontaneous and exciting, just like the good old days. Denise babysat Cassie, and Brad and Carly would dance, party, and make love. Brad's job may have been hard but he always had time and energy for Carly, and she was always ready for him. Her life with Brad was so secure and happy, and Cassie brought her so much joy that maybe it was time to give her a little brother or sister. The thought never crossed her mind that Brad wasn't thinking the same as her.

CHAPTER SEVEN

Baby Ann

It was amazing how the move changed Brad, even the holidays were full of family and fun. Now more than ever Carly wanted another baby. Months went by and in April Carly started to feel a little queasy in the mornings. "Hey, Hon," Brad said to Carly, "You've been looking a little peaked lately, and what's with the sleepiness? Are you coming down with something?"

"I have no idea, maybe it's the flu."

"Well if you're not feeling better in a few days, I want you to go to the doctor and get a checkup."

Brad's concern touched Carly. "Okay, chief, I'll get a checkup if I don't feel better in a week." The thought never crossed her mind that her baby wishes had come true. Carly called the doctor and made an appointment. It was time for her yearly checkup anyway, so why not kill two birds with one stone? Thanks to a cancellation, Carly got an appointment for the next day. With Cassie in hand, she drove to the doctors office and signed in. She took a seat, still felling a little queasy and a little lightheaded. "Mrs. Stevenson, the doctor will see you now," a nurse said as she pulled open a door for Carly to walk through.

Carly was actually happy to go in, she really felt lousy. "Hello Carly, what seems to be the problem?" Dr. Rothman asked.

"I feel queasy, lightheaded, irritable, and very tired. Do you think that I have the flu?"

Dr. Rothman chuckled, "Carly, did it ever occur to you that you might be pregnant?"

Carly's eyes got as big as quarters. "Well, I'll be damned, how stupid could I be? Do you really think it's possible?" She asked with great excitement.

"Let's do an exam and find out. Get up on the table and we'll check things out."

As Carly got up on the table, she could hardly contain her joy. Now that her life with Brad was going so well, a new baby would be the icing on the cake to complete her happiness and dreams. "Well doc, what do you think?"

"Why don't you put your clothes on and meet me in my office." Carly almost leapt off the table as she hurried to get dressed. She knocked on the door and entered Dr. Rothmans office. She sat down across the desk from the doctor and anxiously awaited the news. Dr. Rothman leaned back in his chair and smiled. "Looks like I'll be seeing you on a regular basis. You're going to have a baby in December."

Carly reached from across the desk and grabbed his hands. "Thank you so much, you've made me so happy!"

"Don't thank me," he laughed, "thank your husband. I'll get your prescriptions ready and you make your next appointment for one month. Now get plenty of rest." He walked Carly to the door and told her congratulations.

The nurse at the front desk had kept Cassie occupied. Carly came into the waiting room and Cassie asked, "Mommy, are you okay?"

"Yes honey, I'm just fine. I just found out that you're going to have a little brother or sister." Her feet hardly touched the ground as she left the doctors office, she couldn't wait to get home and tell Brad. Carly called Denise and asked if Cassie could sleep over her house that night. Denise said sure, but asked why. "I just have something I need to talk to Brad about and I want to be alone to talk with him." Denise was confused, but came over and got Cassie. Before Denise arrived, Carly told Cassie, "Remember what we talked about at the doctors about a new brother or sister?" Cassie nodded her head yes. "Well, for now that's our little secret. Don't say anything to Grandma, okay?"

"Ok mommy, but can I tell my doll?"

Carly smiled and said, "Sure honey, just don't tell Grandma." Carly waved to Cassie and Denise as they left. The excitement was more than she could hold in. Brad would be home at eleven thirty. She had enough time to get ready for him and plan her surprise.

Brad normally had a great time at work, but not that day. He usually worked night turn, a shift he was comfortable with. That day he came in for a three to eleven o'clock shift. It was a lot busier on that shift and he was exhausted. For the first time in a long time, he just wanted to go out after work and drink, but he fought the urge and changed his mind to go home to Carly. He hoped everything was fine from her doctor appointment. *It's probably just the flu, it's been going around,* he thought to himself as he drove home. And to be honest, he was too tired to go out anywhere.

Carly made a small romantic late dinner for Brad. She lit some candles and placed them around the living room. She put on some soft music and waited to tell Brad the good news. Brad pulled into the driveway and Carly's heart skipped a beat. Brad walked through the front door and was puzzled. "Hey Carly, what's with the candles?"

Carly just laughed, "Come on, can't a girl get romantic with her favorite guy?"

Brad was all confused now. "I thought you were sick, what did the doctor say?"

Carly put her arms around his neck, looked straight into his eyes, and said, "Oh, I'll be just fine . . . in about eight months." Then she kissed him on the lips.

Brad pulled her arms off his neck and said, "What do you mean you'll be okay in eight months?"

Carly laughed, "Silly, we're going to have a baby!"

Brad's face turned white. "I thought we agreed one was enough?"

Brad's reaction was making Carly very nervous. "Brad we've been so happy and I just wanted to give Cassie a brother or sister."

"But what about me, what about my feelings? You didn't even

talk to me about this." Brad was beside himself with frustration. Just when he had gotten adjusted to and enjoyed family life as it was, Carly threw this at him. "And what about your health? You know how sick you and Cassie were, I don't want that to happen again."

"Dr. Rothman assured me that I'm very healthy and should have no problem with having a healthy baby. Please be happy Brad, everything will be fine." No matter how much Carly wished it to be true, nothing was ever fine again.

Carly had foolishly let her guard down. She loved Brad so much. She thought that he had gotten all of his partying out of his system in California. She was wrong and soon found that his partying days had only just begun.

Her pregnancy again was strenuous. As much as she loved having children, in her heart, she knew that her body would only be able to give birth twice. Even more stressful was the pressure from Brad, not to embark on another pregnancy again after this one. After the lengthy labor, Carly finally delivered a little girl, whom she named Ann. About two months after Ann was born, Brad decided to get a vasectomy. He told Carly that for health reasons, she should not have any more children. Carly reluctantly agreed to the procedure. This decision truly opened the door for Brad and what was about to take place. His motives for a vasectomy were not just so that he'd never have to worry about having anymore children with Carly, but also with anyone else.

CHAPTER 8

Let The Games Begin

Carly kept herself busy with her two sweet little girls, while Brad found fun outside the home. Bonding and interacting with his two children just didn't fit into his daily plans. Carly realized that it was easier to spend her life wrapped around her children, than to persuade Brad to take an active role in their family unit. Sometimes she wondered if her life would be better off without Brad then a life with him. Carly tried her best to make an effort to include Brad in family events, but for one reason or another, they always turned into disasters. He would disappoint his children by not showing up or if he did, he was drunk. Cassie and Ann may have been too young to understand the problems that their parents were encountering, but they weren't too young to feel the pains of an unresponsive father.

Brad allowed the girls to fit into his life on a limited basis. On good days, probably when he needed a break from his wild lifestyle, he'd pay attention to them. But, most of the time, Cassie and Ann missed the daily pleasures of having a loving father in their lives. There were many nights when Ann would sit by her bedroom window and look, watch and wait for daddy to come home. When he didn't, Ann thought it was her fault. She thought that maybe she could have been a better little girl. Cassie on the other hand, held her emotions inside. Her thoughts seemed to be that she had her Mommy, and if Daddy wasn't there, then so be it. As they got older, the kids seemed to understand the problems that Carly and Brad were having. The girls spent more time out of the house when Brad was at home. They felt the pain of having to watch their drunken father argue with Carly. Brad never seemed to care about whom he hurt, just as long as he got what he wanted from that moment; including money, freedom, and no responsibilities.

The years went by, and though some days were good with Brad, most were bad. Carly figured that it was time that she headed back into the work force. She wanted the flexibility to be there when the girls got home from school, so she secured a job in a local flower shop. She had always been very artistic and loved the soft smell of the fragrant flowers. It seemed like a profession custom suited for her. She dreamt of learning enough so that she could eventually open up her own store without any assistance from Brad. Carly worked very hard, and soon one day she had her own shop.

But it was short lived. Brad had started gambling and was now out of control. Financially, they were strapped. Carly took money from her business to try to save their home, but she ended up losing both her business and their home. She was absolutely devastated. Not only did her dream of a life with Brad fade into a memory, but her business aspirations had died as well.

By then, life with Brad had become unbearable. He was drunk almost every day and verbally and physically abusive to Carly and the kids. For Cassie and Ann's sake, it was time to finally ask him to leave. It was a heart breaking separation for Carly. Somewhere deep inside of her, she still loved Brad and longed for their days of long ago. She just couldn't fathom what had gone wrong. If she could only go back to the time when they were deeply in love with one another, but that seemed so long ago.

Carly took another job with a local flower shop, and somehow was able to make ends meet. The bright spot to Brad's absence was that there were no longer any fights. The girls could finally bring friends home without being embarrassed, and Carly was able to get a full nights rest. Carly was attractive and fun to be with, but she never took advantage of being free from Brad. In the back of her mind, she thought that if Brad spent enough time away from his family, that he would miss them and return home again sober.

Brad wasn't stupid either; he kept in touch with Carly. He was having a great time in his life without her, but the money was flowing out his pockets faster then he could replace it. He gave Carly a small amount of money every month for Cassie and Ann, but it was never on time and never enough. It took him a lot of money to support his own lifestyle. Brad worked hard to earn that money, but he played even harder. He knew how to get into Carly's heart and after four years, he did just that.

Love is blind, and so was Carly when it came to Brad. He had gotten tired of jumping from woman to woman, and was running out of money in the process. Carly began a new job as a personal assistant to an executive, and Brad smelled money. Brad began to send sweet cards and called every day to see how work was. He was the king of getting what he wanted and once again, Carly fell for his antics. No matter how hard she tried time and time again, she could never get over Brad. He was like a poison, a deadly drug that an addict craves, which slowly began to ruin their lives.

Just before their fortieth birthdays, they got back together. They moved closer to the hospital into a beautiful condominium with a pool, tennis court, and lovely grounds. It seemed to be perfect for the girls and a new life again for Carly. Brad also settled down for a time. The move to a new area, having made new friends, and not drinking, transposed him into the old Brad that Carly fell in love with years ago.

Even the girls were happy. He still liked to gamble, but Carly figured that he was at least sober, and allowed this habit to continue. In fact, she even began to gamble with Brad on occasion. She really didn't like to spend money frivolously, but she loved Brad too much to take another chance on losing him again. She wanted to lighten up, and be Brad's lover and friend again. Yet trying to be everything to Brad was taking its toll on her financially. In order for Carly to give him the money that he needed to gamble, Carly had to work overtime. While she spent long hours at work, the beast in Brad started to rear its ugly head once again.

The changes in Brad were gradual, a little at a time. He desperately needed money and he couldn't take the chance of pissing Carly off, since she was his major source of income. Money was his lifeline. If she even had the slightest notion that the vicious cycle was beginning all over again with his drinking and cheating ways, she would cut him off.

CHAPTER NINE

Cassie and Ann Get Married

Cassie grew into a beautiful young woman. She fell in love and got married. Even though Cassie was only twenty, Carly was very happy for her. Somehow, in the back of her mind, Carly wished Cassie would wait, but instead, she gave her approval for the wedding. A year later, Cassie gave birth to a baby girl named Amber. Two years later, she had another child; this one was a bouncing baby boy, which she named Cody.

Brad wasn't a good father and being a grandfather really wasn't up his alley. First of all, he considered himself entirely too young to even think about grandchildren let alone to be a grandfather. He had nothing to do with them. To give any time to them took away from his extra curricular activities and that just wasn't going to happen. Brad needed to have fun and the need for danger and excitement was as powerful now if not more so then when he was younger. The time clock was ticking and Brad started drinking again to drown out the sound of the years slipping away. The disease was coming back, seeping into Carly's life like an overflowing sewer. She wasn't stupid; she could see it coming. The staying out all night, the ill temper, and the drinking, she was watching a monster rise from the dead and she was scared to death.

Ann was the next to get married and leave the house. Her wedding was absolutely beautiful, resembling something out of a California society page. Carly had worked long and hard to make everything perfect. The wedding and reception took place poolside on the most glorious day of the summer. Two hundred and fifty people were invited to attend the ceremony, cocktail party and reception. Amazingly, Carly was able to convince Jack to fly in for the wedding. Now that was a miracle in itself, since he had not come back for Brad and Carly's wedding years ago, he had not been home for about eight years, since his mother died. It was about time.

All the stress of the wedding plans drove Brad over the edge. Money that could have been in his hands was going to pay the wedding bills. By the time the wedding week arrived Brad was sick of it all and didn't hide it. Jack, with his new wife Celeste, stayed with Brad and Carly. Ann had already moved out so they stayed in her old room. If Carly had it to do over again, she would have sent them to a hotel. They would have had a much more peaceful visit. Brad ruined everything. Jack and Celeste were very uncomfortable throughout the whole visit. Brad was ill tempered, reminding everyone of a spoiled little brat. If he wasn't the center of attention, he went off and got drunk. He could do that better than most. Somehow the ceremony went off without a hitch, in spite of Brad.

By the end of the reception, Brad had become totally toasted. He began to make a real ass out of himself. Thank God by that time, Ann and Will had left to go on their honeymoon, so they didn't see him disintegrate into an obnoxious drunk. Jack couldn't wait to go back to California. He looked at Carly and said, "Honey, I don't know why you're staying with him, you must have your reasons; but if I were you, I'd leave before he destroys you." If only Carly would have heeded his advice, she would have had an entirely different life today.

Brad and Jack said their good-byes. The air was so thick you could cut it with a knife. Neither one of them showed any emotion. Jack was over Brad's bad temperament and Brad wanted to get back to having fun without everyone watching his every move.

That day was the beginning of the end of life as Carly ever thought it would be. With Ann out of the house, Brad didn't hold anything back. His demands for money grew, his drinking accelerated, and he started spending more and more time away from Carly. Try as she might, she couldn't even buy his love. Where was all the money going? It was easier to just give him what he wanted then to fight. Their marriage was over, if only Carly would have opened her eyes and seen the writing on the wall.

CHAPTER TEN

Trip to India

With the girls married and on their own; the house had become very empty. Carly had made some close friends, but she never wanted to burden them with her mountain of problems. *How could they help*, she had no idea how a love that had been so strong all those years ago can just wither away and die. This was the time, with the girls gone, that they should be having fun. Yet that was the last thing that they were having.

Carly threw herself into her job. The pay was great and she needed every dime. She had paid for Ann's wedding so that money needed to be replaced and for the first time in a long time, she was facing the reality that someday she might truly be alone. That's not what she wanted, yet she had to face the facts.

Ann gave Carly the big news that she was going to have a baby. The one bright spot in her life was her children and grandchildren. Being a grandma didn't bother Carly at all. She still had a great figure and for forty-eight did not look her age. Being in the business world gave her a newfound confidence; she was not afraid now, to stand on her own two feet.

Carly relished the time away from home. She'd leave Brad money on the table, go to work, and not have to see him. Work was exciting, a business trip was coming up and she was thrilled; it was to India. For two weeks she'd be able to clear her head and make her plans for the future.

"Well, you're finally home," Carly says to Brad as he opened the door.

"Look, you know that I work long hours, besides I need the overtime money." Brad bristled at being questioned.

"Is it new hospital policy to serve beer on the overtime shift?"

Brad turned sharply to her and said, "You know you're so fucking funny I can't stand it! I stopped for a few beers, so what?"

"You know we have to talk about my trip. You'll have to take me to the airport." She was looking for some sign that Brad would miss her, but it wasn't there.

"I'll take you if I can; if I have to work, you're on your own."

"Christ Brad, all I need is a ride to the airport. I'll be gone for two weeks; can you at least pretend that you'll miss me?"

"Carly you're acting like you're going to be gone for a month, it's no big deal, besides, I put in for overtime, so I'll be working the whole time you're gone." After about five more beers, the conversation began to turn ugly. "By the way, you'd better leave me some extra money; I've got to get some work done on my car." Brad would say anything to get money out of Carly.

"What do you mean, 'work done on my car'? We just had it in two months ago and you said it was done for awhile. Do you think I grow dollar bills? I need money to take with me to India!"

"Look asshole, I need money while your gone, I have things I have to take care of."

Carly screamed at Brad, "You have your pay, so use your own money. I'm not leaving you any money to party with. I'm done with that, you're on your own. I'm not your bank anymore! Drink and gamble with your own goddamn money!"

"You're nothing but a selfish little bitch," Brad yelled at the top of his lungs to Carly. "No wonder I can't stand coming home, you're nothing but a pain in the ass!"

"Well, I hate it when you come home too. All I am to you is a pay check, but the bank is now closed. You've gotten all you're going to get from me; you're not worth the price I'm paying for you! Life with you has been hell all over again and I can't take it anymore. The only reason we got back together was to have a nice life and to be happy. Well, I'm not happy and our life sucks! When I get back from India, if things aren't better, I'm leaving you."

"What do you mean you're leaving?" Brad laughed at her. "You tried that once before and you came running right back to me. You can't make it on your own, you're too weak."

His words cut through Carly's heart like a knife. How could he be so cruel? "I have a good job now, and without the girls to worry about, I'll be just fine, especially when I won't have to give you any more money."

"You don't have what it takes to make it on your own, you're all talk." For the first time, Brad actually was a little concerned that Carly would follow through with her threat and leave. His lifestyle was one that took money, so he decided to shut up and let her cool off. Carly had made up her mind that she was going to leave, and when she came back home, it wouldn't have taken a genius to see that their life together was over.

Brad did take Carly to the airport the next day; they parted coldly. His mind was on Marnie, her mind was on planning a new life. Carly cried softly, not because she would miss Brad, but because she knew he wouldn't miss her.

*   *   *

After leaving the airport Brad rushed off to work to see Marnie. Two wonderful weeks together without having to sneak around. Carly's money kept him alive, and Marnie is what made his life worth living. He got to the hospital and changed into his uniform. They matched their schedules together for the two weeks that Carly would be gone. They would have the same days off, so that they could spend as much time together as possible. Brad was clever, he conveniently didn't tell anyone at the hospital that Carly and him had gotten back together. Most of them assumed that they had gotten a divorce after four years. Yet he still couldn't take any chances; if the 'higher-ups' got wind of anything going on, there'd be big trouble.

When Marnie met Brad in the lounge, he could hardly control himself. "We have two unbelievable weeks together, and tonight will just be a preview of things to come," he whispered into Marnie's ear.

His hot breath on her neck sent a shiver down her spine. "Tonight darling, we'll create magic," she whispered in his ear then gave him an intoxicating purr.

They met each other at their regular motel, same time. As soon as they saw each other, their eyes met and the fire began. The next day, Brad's blood was boiling; he could hardly concentrate at work. He couldn't stop thinking about her. Damn everyone, he was where he wanted to be, with Marnie.

They unleashed their passion with a fury. Unbridled sex; wild, hot, exciting. They pressed their bodies together and made love wildly, it was as if they were the only two people on the face of the earth, and for two weeks that was how they were, wrapped in each other.

*   *   *

Carly arrived in India on schedule. It was twenty-five hours of traveling, but she slept most of the way. She hadn't slept much in the past few weeks; her mind and body needed to rest. India was all she thought it would be and more. Although she was kept very busy, she had time to take in the sights, sounds, and smells of the country. She also made time to think about what she was going to do when she got back home. She would get home two days before Thanksgiving, so after that, she would get an apartment and finally start her new life. It's not what she wanted, but she had no other choice, she was sick to death of trying to buy Brad's love. If he won't give it to her freely, then she didn't want it at all.

Leaving India was tough. Carly had gotten sick the last three days there, and she was exhausted from all the work she had done, and she missed the kids, all of them. The thought of having to face Brad made her even more sick. As much as she wanted to go home, she just didn't want to get into anything with Brad, not yet. She needed to sleep and get her strength back to battle with him. A couple of days would be soon enough.

Brad was on time to pick her up. He wished she would have never come back, but the reality was, he was broke. He had spent money on Marnie like he was rich. Anything she wanted to do, they did. It was the best two weeks of his life, but now he needed cash quickly. The minute Carly looked at Brad; she knew he was there because he had to be, not because he wanted to be. Driving home they barely spoke to each other. The wall between them had gotten higher and wider, and it was evident that she had to leave. As she unpacked from her trip, she felt like re-packing and leaving right then and there, but she was just too tired to fight. She needed a bath and a nice warm bed; tomorrow was always another day.

CHAPTER ELEVEN

Brad's Obsession Grows

Brad left the house telling Carly that he had to go to work, even though he knew he wasn't. His head was spinning and he wanted to be with Marnie, but she was working. So he went to the club and got drunk. The pressures on him were starting to take their toll. His head was pounding. If only he could figure out how to keep Marnie and still get money out of Carly, maybe his headache would go away. How he got home without wrecking the car was a miracle. He was blind, stinking drunk and could hardly walk. He walked though the door and ended up passing out on the couch. When Carly woke up she went into the living room to find Brad passed out on the couch, reeking of beer. *When did he come home?* She thought he was at work. She tried to wake him, which was a big mistake.

"What the fuck are you doing?" he screamed at her.

"Are you okay? I thought you had to go to work."

"Just get the hell away from me; I don't need you bugging me." Too tired to argue, Carly went back to bed and cried herself to sleep.

The whole family was coming over to Carly's house for Thanksgiving dinner. They wanted to hear all about her trip and to see her and Brad. Brad conveniently forgot to tell Carly that he had to work on Thanksgiving until the next morning. She was almost relieved. Family gatherings with Brad usually turned out to be bad, so a peaceful holiday was a welcome break. The only two that were disappointed was Jerry, his stepbrother, and Denise, his mother. They didn't get to come over too often and they wanted to see Brad. The house was full; Carly loved having everyone there. The house was so empty most of the time, that it was nice to hear laughter. This gave Carly a chance to talk to Jerry in private. He knew how unhappy she had been and sensed that something was about to happen.

Carly pulled Jerry into a room and spoke to him softly, "Jerry, I'm leaving Brad, I can't take it anymore, and he's become unbearable to live with. I'll need your help to find an apartment and move. Please say that you'll help me, I just can't do this alone."

"You know that whatever and whenever you need me, I'll be there. You've tried so hard to keep your family together, and I'm sure that if you thought there was any hope, you'd stay."

Carly could hardly get the words out, "I'm afraid that with the way Brad's been drinking, he's either going to have a heart attack or a stroke. And with my luck he'll have a stroke and I'll be the one left in the mud taking care of him, and I don't want to do that. That probably sounds selfish, but I need a life too."

"That's not being selfish, that's being honest and I can understand your concern. I'm worried about him myself."

Carly had finally taken the first step to start her new life and she felt great about her decision. With Jerry's help, maybe she'd be able to move out before Christmas; that way the grandchildren could sleep over, something they hadn't been able to do. But that wasn't to be.

When Denise found out about what Carly had in mind, she was crushed. "How could you do that at Christmas? Can't you at least wait until after the New Year to leave? Just let me have one more Christmas with our whole family together, please, Carly, please," she begged.

How could Carly turn her down, Denise's second husband Sam had just died fourteen months earlier, and the desperation in her voice broke Carly's heart. "Okay, Mom, I'll wait, but only until after the New Year, then I have to leave."

Again, she was trapped, but maybe this was an omen to try just one more time to win back Brad's love. She had waited this long, so what was another couple of months? If only she could have seen into the future, she would have left right then and never looked back.

Brad had to work Christmas Eve, which gave Carly a chance to put her plan into action. She had bought a beautiful negligee in red, Brad's favorite color. She filled the house with scented candles, chilled a bottle of champagne, put on some soft music, and waited anxiously for Brad to come home.

*   *   *

Brad only worked half of his three to eleven shift; he had plans to be with Marnie. He wouldn't be able be see her Christmas Day, because he would have to be home with Carly and the family. The thought of spending all day at home made him sick to his stomach, but he had to keep Carly from getting suspicious. She already had cut off some of the money that she gave him, and the credit card bills were pilling up. Maybe if he could get through Christmas without fighting with her, she might loosen her purse strings. He had to try.

Marnie had plans of her own for Brad. She knew that they would only have a few hours together, so she wasted no time getting things ready for Brad's arrival. All she was wearing was a giant bow tied around her waist. She would give him a present that he wouldn't be quick to forget. They spent their few hours wrapped in each other's arms. It would be one whole week until they would be able to see each other again this way, so they didn't want to waste a single minute. He had to go straight home after being with Marnie; he had promised Carly that he would be home as soon as possible. It was hard to leave Marnie, but to keep some kind of peace at home he had to go.

"I'll try to see you at work tomorrow. I'll come in early before your shift is done. It'll be tough to get away, but don't leave until I get there." Brad leaned down to the bed and kissed Marnie long and hard. He didn't want the night to end, but he had to leave.

"I love you Brad. You'll be in my heart, even if you're not in my arms tonight." Tears rolled softly down her cheeks as she said good-bye.

At midnight, Brad arrived home. He stood outside the house not wanting to go in. This wasn't where he wanted to be, but he had no choice. He entered the house hoping that Carly would have already gone to bed, but that wasn't what he found. Carly greeted Brad with a long passionate kiss. It took him off guard. They hadn't been together in months and this was the last thing he had expected. "What's gotten into you?" he asked with shock still apparent in his eyes.

"I know that we haven't been together for months, but I do still love you Brad, and I'd like to try and start over. We were happy once, you and I, can't we give our life together one more chance?"

"Carly, I'm so tired from work; I'm not really up for this."

"Let me give you a back rub like I used to, maybe that will get things started." Carly wasn't going to give up without a fight. It was all or nothing now.

"Let me take a shower first; I didn't get to take one before I left the hospital." Brad was scrambling for a way out of this mess. Even if he wanted to, which he didn't, he was spent. Marnie had drained every last drop of energy out of him, and he would never be able to get it up. Carly poured the wine and did everything she could to try to arouse Brad, but it was no use, there was nothing there for her anymore. That night, Carly closed the bedroom door and never opened it to him again. It was time to go.

CHAPTER TWELVE

Baby Dakota

Christmas Day was cold outside and even colder inside. Everyone came over. Family and friends were in and out all day long. Carly smiled, laughed and joked with everyone, but in her heart, she was crying. If it hadn't been clear before, it was clear now: Brad didn't love her anymore.

Carly's plans to leave were once again prolonged. Carly threw herself into her work. The long hours kept her out of the house until late at night. By then, either Brad had gone to work, or he had passed out drunk on the couch. They hardly ever talked anymore, which suited Carly just fine. She was looking forward to the birth of Ann's baby. Ann was due in May, so in March, Cassie and Carly planned a baby shower for Ann. It was an exciting time for a lot of reasons. Carly decided that she would leave Brad after Ann had the baby. She didn't want to upset Ann now in her condition. Besides, a move in the spring would be much easier than a move in the winter.

Brad was spinning out of control. His workload at the hospital had doubled due to cutbacks in staff. If he wasn't working, he was with Marnie, and when he wasn't with Marnie, he was out drinking and gambling. His headaches were becoming more frequent, so he drank even more to numb the pain. His insatiable need to be with Marnie sapped all his energy. He didn't eat right and he wasn't sleeping enough. He looked like hell. He had been warned numerous times by his supervisor to clean up his act, but he just didn't care anymore.

He was determined to do things his way, no matter what the consequences. When he was with Marnie nothing else in the world mattered. His appetite for her was overwhelming. The more he saw her, the more he desired her. Money had now become a real problem. His credit cards had reached their limit and Carly had stopped giving him cash. The problems were just beginning for Brad. He should have slowed down, but it was too late. The downward spiral had begun, and there was nothing left to break his fall.

On May 8th Ann went into labor. Everyone went to the hospital to be with her and Will. Carly, Cassie, Amber, and Will's mother Donna were all there to help coach Ann along. Choosing a midwife to deliver the baby allowed Carly and Donna to have an active part in the delivery. The miracle of birth is something that cannot be described in words. It is so spiritual when a new life arrives; it renews the soul and spirit of everyone that is a witness to it. Brad was not there, because being a part of anything dealing with his family cramped his lifestyle. His lack of interest hurt Ann deeply. She longed for her father's love. Yet Brad was too self-centered and cold to give love to anyone but Marnie.

Ann and baby boy Dakota came home from the hospital within a few days time. Carly was so busy helping Ann getting settled in her home, that she had no time to think about Brad. Between work and helping Ann, Carly barely had time to change her clothes. Her children and grandchildren gave her so much joy; something that Brad would never experience. How sad for him, "If Dad would only take five minutes to see the baby, maybe that wall he's built around himself would come down," Ann told Carly on the phone.

"Why don't you come over with the baby on Saturday, he may be home." Carly hoped that the meeting would open the door between Ann and her father. She just prayed that Brad would be sober when they arrived.

"O.k., Mom, we'll give it a try. I just hope Dad is sober when we get there."

There was never a lack of drinking buddies for Brad. The guys at the apartment complex loved to sit around and pound down the beers. Someone would always have an ample supply to go around. That Saturday, Brad didn't come home from his night turn shift until about noon. He was already feeling no pain from drinking. Carly begged him not to drink because Ann and the baby were coming over. She could see that her pleas had fallen upon deaf ears. He went over to his friend Dom's place and continued to get drunk. Carly tried to call Ann and stop her from coming over, but she had already left. A cold chill ran up her spine. She prayed that she could convince Ann to come back another day, but it was too late. Ann's car pulled up the driveway just as Brad staggered out of the neighbor's apartment.

She put the baby in the stroller and walked over to her father. "I thought that you might want to see your new grandson," she said to Brad.

"Oh yeah, he's real cute," Brad slurred. "Hey Dom, get me another beer. Never mind, I'll come in and get it myself." With that, he turned around and left Ann standing there as she watched her father stagger away from both her and his new grandson, Dakota.

Ann was heartbroken and told Carly, "I'm done with him Mom. How can he be so cold? Doesn't he have a heart? This is his grandson, and he couldn't care less." Tears began to stream down her face. This time Brad had hurt her for the last time. "I love you Mom, but I won't come over here again if he's here. I don't ever want to see him again!"

"I'm so sorry honey, I tried to stop you, but you had already left. I didn't want you to go through this," Carly explained to her weeping daughter.

"What's the difference Mom? He'll never change, and the sooner you leave, the better off you'll be. How do you put up with him? He is a waste of life! Get on with your life Mom, and get rid of him!" Ann screamed, hoping that he would have heard her, but no such luck, as if it would have mattered even if he had heard.

Carly confessed, "I was waiting until after you had Dakota to make my plans. In June, there will be a one-bedroom apartment open, and I'm taking it. When I get my next pay, I am going to put down a deposit on it."

"Just make sure that you leave this time, don't let him change your mind." Ann said as she gave her Mom a big hug.

Ann's visit convinced Carly that it was, indeed, time to make her move. Soon she would be rid of him and regain control of her life. Yet nothing in the world could have prepared Carly for what was about to happen. On May 29th, the chain reaction that Brad had started would explode right in her face.

CHAPTER THIRTEEN

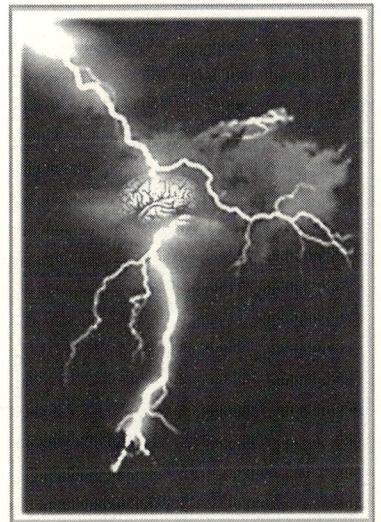

Carly was planning a Memorial Day picnic by the pool for the kids, Jerry and Denise, along with some other friends. Brad told her that he had to work a double shift, so he wouldn't be home for the entire weekend. He hadn't been home much the last few days anyway, but at least she knew that he wouldn't pop in and ruin the picnic. Carly called everyone, and they were all coming. The forecast predicted a beautiful, warm day. Carly was off from work for the entire weekend. Maybe for the first time in a long while she would be able to relax and actually have a little fun.

Work had been hectic lately, but the overtime money would help in her move. However, Carly was very tired; the strain of work and having to deal with Brad had drained her physically as well as emotionally. This weekend would hopefully afford her a much needed rest.

Carly left work early on Friday and anticipated a restful holiday. She normally would have worked until eight p.m., but she arrived home at five o'clock that day. She pulled up into her driveway, saw Brad's car and thought to herself, *Oh, great. Just what I need, a confrontation with him.* She opened the door and found no sign of Brad anywhere. *He's probably at Dom's getting drunk. He'd better stop soon; he's got to work tonight. He'll have to eat and sober up before he leaves.*

At around seven o'clock, Brad staggered in through the door, more drunk than usual. Carly asked him, "Don't you think that you should have stopped drinking a little earlier? You have to go to work tonight." His condition and look on his face frightened her.

"What the hell do you care? If I want to get drunk, that's my business! Just shut the fuck up and leave me alone," Brad screamed back at her almost spitting in her face.

Ice formed in Carly's stomach. His eyes starred through her with a cold, hateful glare. "Look," Carly screamed right back at him, "I really don't give a shit about how much you drink anymore, but you're going to lose your job if you go to work drunk like this. You've been warned, and next time you'll be fired!"

"Who the fuck do you think you are, telling me what to do? Just because you're some high and mighty personal assistant doesn't mean that you can tell me how to handle my job! You think you know everything, but you know nothing. I won't get fired!" Brad screamed back in Carly's face, spraying her with his drunken foul breath. By then, Brad could hardly stand up and he began to stagger back and forth.

This is bad, real bad, Carly said to herself quietly. *Maybe he'll pass out. Then I can call him off work sick. That is better than him showing up drunk.* Brad finally collapsed, half of his body on the floor and the other half on the sofa. Carly waited to be sure that he was out cold then said aloud, "In about ten minutes I'm going to call you off." As Carly walked over to the phone to call the hospital, it rang.

"Hello. This is the staffing office at County General Hospital; may I please speak with Brad?"

Carly's heart jumped. "He's sleeping right now, he's not feeling very well, can I help you?"

"We need Brad to come in as soon as possible, there's been an emergency, may I speak with him?"

Oh great, how the hell am I going to sober him up in time to go into work? her mind raced. "Look, I'll do my best to get him up, but he may be late."

"That's fine; just make sure that he leaves as soon as possible."

Carly's hands were shaking as she hung up the phone. How in the hell was she going to wake him up? Brad had a bad temper when he was drunk, and waking him up now could be dangerous; he may become violent. She leaned over and shook him. "Brad, the hospital just called, you have to go to work, there's been an emergency. Please Brad, get up, you're going to get into trouble." Carly was trembling.

Brad started to stir and mumbled incoherently, throwing his arms wildly in the air. "Get away from me you bitch! What the fuck are you doing? Leave me alone!"

"Come on, please, get up, I'll make you some coffee and something to eat. I just don't want you to get into trouble." By now, Carly was frantic; she just didn't want him to get violent.

He pulled himself up from the couch and pushed her to the floor. "I told you to leave me the fuck alone. I'll leave when I'm goddamn ready to leave, so stay the fuck out of my face or I'll knock you out!"

"How can you do this to me?" she screamed, "I'm just trying to save your ass." Carly was crying and shaking, she was terrified by the look on his face. Brad walked to the bedroom to get ready and passed out on the bed. Panic-stricken, Carly called Lindsey,

Dom's wife. "Lindsey, can you have Dom come over and get Brad up for work? He's really drunk and I'm afraid of him."

"Are you kidding? Dom's just as drunk as Brad. He's passed out on the bed. Don't do anything foolish, just let him sleep."

"I can't," Carly told Lindsey, "The hospital called and wants him there right now, there's an emergency."

"Well good luck and be careful. I know how he can get when he's drunk."

Carly hung up the phone and called to Brad from the bottom of the stairs. "Brad, come on, get moving, you're going to get fired, please get up."

"I'm up goddamn it, I'm getting dressed. Now quit flapping your mouth." Brad came down the stairs with a smirk on his face. "You think you know everything, well you don't. Trust me, you don't have a goddamn clue, in fact, you're the dumbest bitch I have ever met in my entire life." As Brad left, he looked back at Carly and laughed, "What a fucking loser you are."

Carly crumbled into the chair sobbing uncontrollably. She picked up the phone and called Jerry. His answering machine picked up and Carly left a message, "Jerry, it's me, tomorrow when you come over, we'll make plans to get me the hell out of here. I can't take it anymore." She hung up the phone, and she fell asleep in her bed, exhausted. Thank God he had to work a double shift. How he'd do it, she didn't know, but she didn't care, just so long as she didn't have to look at his face or hear his voice. With any luck, she'd be able to get out by Monday, then she could file for a divorce and end this long nightmare.

*   *   *

Marnie was getting really worried as she waited for Brad to show up; he had been late before, but not this late. She had never called his house until now, and hopefully Carly wasn't suspicious. She missed Brad so much, she would do anything to make sure they were together.

How Brad drove to the motel without having an accident was a miracle. He was so drunk that he could hardly walk let alone drive, but his lust and passion for Marnie drove him to take the chance. Marnie ran to the door when she heard Brad, "Oh God, honey, I thought you'd never get here. Are you okay? I've missed you so much and I didn't think that you were coming."

"I'm drunk, but nothing can stop me from being with you. Now get over here so I can bang the hell out of you! You know how beer affects me; I'm horny as hell." He kissed Marnie rougher, harder and with more passion than she had expected. He had to go to work in the morning so he wasted no time. Marnie's long blonde hair fell softly on his face as she mounted him. Her slim legs wrapped around his waist as she rocked him into ecstasy. He held onto her round full breasts and kissed them long and hard. He was rougher with her than usual, but Marnie loved it. They reached their climax together and slipped breathlessly into each other's arms. Within minutes, they both fell fast asleep, holding on to each other, never wanting to let go.

Marnie's portable alarm clock went off at about six a.m. Brad had to be at work for his seven-to-three shift, which gave him plenty of time to get to the hospital. "Brad, honey, its time to get up." No response, "Come on baby, rise and shine." Still no response, "You can't be that tired." Marnie started to get concerned. Brad was hard to wake up, but not this hard.

"Come on, Brad, you've got to get moving," Brad still didn't move. "Brad! Brad! Oh, God! Brad, what's wrong? Honey, please!" Marnie was panic-stricken. Brad finally tried to get up, fell to the floor, and hit his head on the nightstand. He tried to speak, but everything was garbled. Marnie started to scream, "Oh God! Brad, what's wrong, what's happening to you? Don't move, I'll call an ambulance." She could hardly talk when she contacted the main desk of the motel. "Hurry, please call 911, Brad's in trouble, I don't know what's wrong, please hurry."

She threw on her clothes and covered Brad with a blanket. He was shaking and trying to talk but the words just wouldn't come out. Marnie tried to comfort him but he had a blank look in his eyes that scared her to death. The ambulance arrived and the paramedics entered the room.

"Can you tell us what happened?"

"I don't know," Marnie cried, "I tried to wake him up and when he tried to stand, he fell and hit his head on the nightstand. All he does is mumble and shake. Oh God, please help him!"

"Did he take any drugs?"

"No, he was pretty drunk last night, but he was fine when he fell asleep." The medics put Brad on oxygen and loaded him into the ambulance. Marnie climbed into the back with Brad. The ambulance had the lights flashing and sirens roaring as they tore through traffic. She sat next to Brad and put her hand on his forehead, he looked gray and didn't move at all.

"What's wrong with him? Why can't he move or talk, will he be okay?" Marnie was crying so hard that the paramedics could hardly understand her. "The only thing we can tell you is that we think he had a stroke. How bad of one, we do not know. Right now, we just want to make him stable."

"The hospital is ready for our arrival; they'll take good care of him, just try to calm down."

Marnie couldn't calm down, her whole life was lying on a stretcher fighting for his life, and her life was crumbling right before her eyes. Little did she know that her life would never be same again. It had already changed forever.

CHAPTER FOURTEEN

The Drama Begins

The morning of May 30th was beautiful. The sun was bright, the breeze light, the trees were showing bright green leaves and the flowers were in full bloom. It was a perfect day for a picnic by the pool. The weather may have been perfect, but Carly felt like shit. She had tossed and turned all night long; thinking about what had transpired the evening before. The one thing that she was sure of was that as of today, she was going to start her new life. It wasn't the life that she wanted but it had become clear to her that she had to leave before something awful happened. The change in Brad for the worse, had made the decision for her. Before she lost her sanity or her life, she had to go.

It was nine a.m. and Carly was in the kitchen preparing for the picnic. Seeing Ann and Dakota would lift her spirits. Amber and Cody had another picnic to go to and Cassie had to work, but they were going to be over later in the evening for a late night swim. Ann would be happy that Carly had made up her mind to leave. The strain that Carly had endured lately showed and even make-up couldn't cover up the dark circles under her eyes. Ann had been telling her that for months; maybe after leaving Carly would finally get the chance to get a good night's sleep.

The doorbell rang and Carly opened the door, "Hi Ken, you're up early on your day off. What's up?" It was Carly's next-door neighbor.

"Carly is it okay if Mandy and I come down to the pool and join your picnic? I'll bring the hot dogs."

"Sure, Ken, the more the merrier; besides, I can use all the company I can get."

"You and Brad have a bad night last night? You look beat."

"Ken, everything's a mess. I'm leaving Brad as soon as possible, maybe as soon as Monday. I've just had it. I just can't take it, I can't live like this anymore."

"Well, if you need any help, just give a holler. Mandy and I would be glad to give you a hand, we know it's been rough on you."

"Thanks, Ken. Now, no more talk of Brad and me, we have a picnic to get ready for, so I'll see you and Mandy at noon." All of her friends have been so supportive, never judgmental, and for that, she was very grateful. No matter how she felt today, she was determined to have a good time; the company would keep her spirits high, and their support would ease her pain.

As Carly was preparing for Ann and the baby to arrive, she was unaware of the events that were taking place at the hospital at the very same time. Those were the events that were going to change her and everyone else's lives forever. The explosion from the chain reaction that Brad and Marnie had started was now enveloping her, too.

*   *   *

Marnie entered the hospital in a fog. Brad was incoherent and unable to answer any questions or sign any papers. The affair that they had kept secret for so long was now exposed for the whole world to see; what the hell was she going to do? The head nurse came over to Marnie and asked, "Marnie, what happened?"

Marnie nearly collapsed right in her arms. "Oh God, I don't know. They said Brad had a stroke; he can't even talk or stand. That's all I know, I'm so scared!"

By now, the nurse was confused. "How, I mean, why are you with him, what's going on?"

Well, it was too late now for Marnie to lie, so she told Sandy everything. "Brad and I have been seeing each other for months; I never expected anything like this to happen. I don't know what I'm suppose to do!"

"Well the first thing that you have to do is get a hold of yourself. You're not going to help him by being hysterical. Let me get you a glass of water and an aspirin."

Marnie sat down and tried to compose herself. *Okay, Marnie, think. What are you going to do? You're in deep shit now,* she thought to herself.

The nurse came back over to Marnie and asked her to fill out the admission forms. "Marnie, you're going to have to tell me exactly what happened. It's important to try and remember everything." Marnie told her that Brad had been very drunk and that he probably had smoked about three packs of cigarettes the day before. When she tried to wake him up that morning, he couldn't talk. Also, when he tried to get up from the bed, he fell and hit his head on the nightstand. "What are they doing to Brad? Can I go in and be with him? He's probably wondering where I am."

"Brad's in good hands, besides, you have to sign his admission papers, since he's unable to do so."

Marnie's hands were trembling as she signed her name. *My God I've just let the whole world know that I was the one who was with Brad when he was brought to the hospital,* her mind spun with fear.

Sandy put the admission form with Brad's chart. After talking with the doctor, told Marnie, "Honey, they have taken Brad up for a CT scan, he's in pretty bad shape. He's on oxygen, glucose, and antivant, and if he didn't have a bleed in his brain, he will be put on heparin to thin his blood out, to prevent another stroke. He'll be up there for a while, so if you have to call someone, you could do it now. Does Brad have anyone that we should contact?"

Christ, I knew someone was going to ask me that, she thought to herself. "I better make the call myself. I'll call his daughter; I don't have her number here." Sandy agreed that she should try to do that quickly. Marnie sat down in a chair in the waiting room and put her head in her hands. Suddenly she felt a hand on her shoulder; it was Fred, one of the technicians that knew Brad and Marnie.

"Honey, what the hell's going on? I just heard about Brad, and that you were the one who brought him in."

"Fred, it's too complicated to get into, but I really need your help. I have to get his clothes and bring his car up here, but I need a ride, can you help me, please?"

She was sobbing so hard that Fred could hardly turn her down. "Marnie, give me ten minutes. I'll punch out and come down to get you."

She waited anxiously for Fred to meet her outside. He met her after a few long minutes and they left to go to the motel. "I'll explain everything to you tomorrow, right now, I just have to think about my next step," she told Fred as they drove to the motel.

"You don't have to tell me anything, just be careful, whatever you do."

Fred waited for her until she got into the room, the room that she had shared with Brad. She fell onto the bed and cried uncontrollably. The love of her life was lying helpless in the hospital with a stroke. *What should I do next? Think!* There had to be someone she could call. There was no way that she would call Carly. What if she asked questions, what if she would recognize her voice? Marnie didn't want to take that chance; there was no way that she would be able to have a confrontation with Carly right now. She looked through Brad's wallet and found Cassie's phone number. She gathered her thoughts and dialed the number.

"Hello, may I please speak with Cassie?"

Cassie's husband Steve answered the phone, "I'm sorry she's not in, may I ask who's calling?"

"Well, I'm a friend of hers and I need to speak to her, is there a number where I could possibly reach her?"

"No, she's at work right now and she's not allowed personal phone calls. Can I give her a message?'

Marnie had to let someone know about Brad so she told Steve. "Her father Brad Stevenson has been admitted to County General Hospital with a stroke," she couldn't believe that she was able to say the words without crying.

"How do you know that he had a stroke?"

"I work at the hospital and was there when he was bought in. That's all the information I have. Please tell Cassie to get to the hospital as quickly as possible." Marnie hung up the phone before he could ask any more questions. He'll probably call Cassie and then she'll call Carly. She gathered up Brad's clothes and had Fred follow her to the hospital in her car, as she drove Brad's. She breathed in the smell of his car; the scent of his after-shave still lingered. Tears began to stream down her cheeks; her heart became very heavy. She wanted to be with Brad, she knew that he needed her, but that would have to wait until late at night, when no one would be able to see her check on him. She needed time to think. Brad would get better, he had too, their life together depended on it; her life depended on it.

CHAPTER FIFTEEN

The Mystery Unfolds

Carly had everything ready for the picnic, and she actually was feeling quite good. Maybe the fact that Ann was coming over and would be there soon was the reason for her good mood. Ann could always make her laugh and she needed that today. The rest of the family would be arriving around one o'clock, which gave Carly a chance to help Ann get situated. They could have a drink or two to settle down her nerves.

Ann arrived with Dakota at noon. It was so cute to see her as a mother, juggling diaper bags, a stroller, and a play hut. Carly laughed to herself and remembered the days when she had gone through all of that with Ann and Cassie. "Well, honey, do you think you brought enough stuff? He's only three weeks old." Carly laughed as she helped Ann unload her car.

"God, Mom, I can't believe how many things I need just to spend the day out of the house. I feel like a moving company."

Carly could feel the pressure lifting off her shoulders. Seeing the baby, that new little life, renewed her faith. Carly and Ann wheeled Dakota down to the pool; Ken and Mandy were already there waiting for them.

"Boy, am I glad to see you guys. I could sure use the help getting the baby set up."

Ken started laughing and jumped right in to help. "Don't worry about anything. Remember, Mandy and I are old pros at this." Ken and Mandy had two grown sons, so helping Ann with the baby was a snap for them.

"Hey Mom, why don't you go back to the house and get the beer, and chips? I could sure use it about now."

"Okay, you stay here with Ken and Mandy, I'll be only a minute." Carly reached the house just in time to hear the phone ring.

"Hello Carly it's Steve, is Brad around?"

"No Steve, he won't be home all day, he's doubling out at the hospital, what's up?"

It was strange that Steve would call Brad, Steve never really liked him. "Carly, Brad's in the hospital, they think he had a stroke."

Carly almost dropped the phone. "Wait a minute, how did you find out? I've been home all day and no one called me." By now, Carly's knees were shaking and she had to sit down, "Please tell me what's going on."

"A woman called from the hospital and asked for Cassie. When I told her that she was at work, she told me about Brad. Look Carly, I'm already on my way to get Cassie, get ready and I'll come by and pick you up too. I don't want you to drive, you sound too upset."

Steve was right about that; it was more like she was in shock. "Okay, Steve, I'll be ready when you get here." Carly ran back to the pool to tell Ann. "Ann, Steve just called, something about your Dad having a stroke and that he is in the hospital. You take care of things here; wait for Jerry and Grandma. Steve's on his way here with Cassie, so we can all go."

"I hope you're not going to drive yourself to the hospital, I think you're too upset Mom. Wait here for Steve; let him take you, please." Ann was more concerned about Carly than she was about Brad; she could see the fear on Carly's face.

"Ann, why didn't the hospital call me? I was home all morning. I don't even know what time it happened." The questions started coming as she decided that she would drive, "Well, I'll wait for Steve and Cassie, but I'm taking my own car, it's only five minutes away. I'll be okay."

"Mom, just be careful, and call me the minute you know anything," Cassie said as they walked outside.

Ken told Carly, "Don't worry about what's going on here, Mandy and I will take care of everything. You just go to the hospital and find out what the hell is going on."

Steve and Cassie pulled up just as Carly came out of the house. "Steve, I'm taking my own car, and I won't take no for an answer. If I have to leave for any reason, I want to be able to go."

Steve wasn't happy with the idea, but he could see that Carly had made up her mind, so he agreed. The whole drive to the hospital, Carly was questioning the reason why the hospital never called her. "They have our phone number, hell, they called Brad into work all the time, so why not a phone call now?" she began talking to herself aloud. *And where did this happen? If it happened in the hospital, surely, someone would have thought to call her,* she thought to herself, confused and afraid of the answers that she might find.

Steve and Carly pulled up to the ER and he told Carly, "Park your car in the patient spot and I'll park it for you in the visitors lot. You go in and see what's going on, we'll be in as soon as possible."

Carly agreed; she parked her car and ran to the admissions desk. The clerk at the front desk asked if she might help her. "Yes, my name is Carly Stevenson, Brad Stevenson's wife. Someone called and said that my husband was admitted to the Emergency Room this morning. May I go and see him?"

"Brad's not in the ER now, he's been moved to the 5th floor, room 5041."

Gee, if he got a room that fast, then he must not be that bad, she thought to herself. "Thank you, I'll go right up." She waited out in the hallway by the elevators until Steve and Cassie got there. She had decided that they should all go up together. The ride in the elevator was very quiet; no one knew what they were going to face once they walked into Brad's room. None of them were prepared for what they were about to see.

They entered Brad's room and immediately became aware that

Brad's condition was severe. There were monitors and IV's and he was breathing on oxygen. It was like they had walked into a nightmare. The nurse was checking Brad's blood pressure as Carly walked into the room. The nurse asked, "May I help you?"

"I'm Mrs. Stevenson; can you tell me how my husband is doing? I received a phone call that he was here and I don't know what's going on."

"Mrs. Stevenson, as far as I know the doctors think that Brad has had a massive stroke. The extent of the damage won't be clear for a while, but he is comfortable, though he's not responding to anyone. Maybe if he hears your voice, he'll react to you."

Carly was overcome with fear. What if he didn't respond to her voice? What if he never recovers? He looked so bad, what if he dies? Carly leaned over the bed and got close to Brad's ear, "Brad, it's me, Carly. Brad, can you hear me, do you know who I am?"

Brad opened his eyes. Carly looked into them but they were void of any response. He had no idea who she was. Carly asked the nurse, "When was he brought up to the 5th floor?"

"At about ten a.m. according to the chart." "Well then, when did this happen?" Carly asked in a confused tone. "The chart shows that he was admitted at around eight a.m." *That didn't make any sense to her, why hadn't they notified her?*

The television was on, and it appeared that Brad was trying to focus on it. "Where are his glasses?" Carly asked the nurse. "Maybe if we put them on him he'll be able to see, he's blind as a bat without them." The nurse told her to look in the closet; his belongings should be there. She and Cassie went to look in the closet. Carly pulled out a plastic bag; all she found in there was his watch, a gold necklace, and a diamond earring.

"There seems to be some items missing," Carly told the nurse. "Where are his clothes, shoes, wallet, and keys to his car?"

"Maybe they're still in the ER. Sometimes they lock the wallets in the closet, I'll call down and check for you." The nurse called down to the ER. "Hi, this is the nurse from the 5th floor; I'm checking on Brad Stevenson's belongings, some of his things are missing." The nurse paused while the person on the other end checked, "I see, well thanks for looking." She turned to Carly, "As far as the ER knows, everything came up with him."

"That's impossible. Someone had to have made a mistake." By now Cassie, Steve, and Carly were totally confused. How could they have lost all his things?

"The only suggestion I have, is that you go downstairs and check for yourself."

The nurse left the room as they looked at one another in disbelief. "Now what?" Carly asked.

"Well, I suggest you and Cassie go to the ER and find out what the hell's going on. I'll stay here in case a doctor comes by or his stuff turns up." Steve sat down while Carly and Cassie headed for the elevators.

"Don't you get the feeling that we've just entered the twilight zone?" Carly asked Cassie on the way downstairs.

"I'll tell you Mom, two and two aren't adding up to make four and I'm getting a real creepy feeling."

"Me too, honey, they'd better have some answers for us at the ER desk or I'll be real pissed off. It's not like your Dad's a stranger, Christ he works here."

Carly could feel the hairs on the back of her neck start to bristle; someone had better know something soon. Nothing was adding up. Little did she know, that nothing was ever going to add up again.

CHAPTER SIXTEEN

Things Get Crazy

The desk at the ER was busy; it was hard for them to get someone's attention. "Excuse me," Carly said to the desk clerk, "my name is Carly Stevenson, my husband Brad was brought here earlier this morning and I need the rest of his belongings."

The nurse looked over to the two women standing in front of her desk and said, "As we told the nurse, all of his things were sent up with him to the fifth floor."

"That can't be. All that's up there is his watch, an earring, and a necklace. Where are his shoes, clothes, wallet, and car keys?"

"Hold on a second. Let me get the supervisor for you, maybe she can help you."

Carly and Cassie watched as the clerk talked to the supervisor. They were huddled around each other in a deep conversation. "What the hell's the big mystery," Cassie asked her Mom, "How can you loose someone else's property?"

"I don't know, and what's the big pow-wow about? I'm beginning to feel very uneasy," Carly said to Cassie as she watched in total bewilderment.

The supervisor came over to them and asked Carly, "Excuse me, who did you say you were?"

"My name is Carly Stevenson, Brad's wife," Carly said firmly to the woman standing in front of her with questioning eyes.

"Well, I wasn't on duty when Brad was brought in, but I understand that he was brought in by ambulance and that he was in his underwear. His wife was the one who admitted him."

Carly felt the blood drain from her face; ice formed in her stomach. She had heard the words, but she couldn't yet grasp the meaning of them. His underwear, his wife? It took her a minute to compose herself. Cassie spoke up louder, "Look lady, this is his wife, and I'm his daughter. You better give us more information than what you already have."

Carly collected her thoughts and calmly told the supervisor, "Alright, here's what I need. Somewhere out there, are his clothes, money, and car. I need to know how to find them. If you can't help me, then tell me who can; I need answers now." Carly thought to herself, *that son of a bitch has really done it this time. How could he be so stupid?*

"The only people that can help you are the EMS. I have their number right here. You can use the phone on my desk; you'll have privacy back there," the woman said as she led them back to her office.

Privacy, it was a little late for that now. Everyone in the ER was straining to hear the entire scoop. The news would soon travel through the whole hospital like wild fire, with her stuck right in the middle of it all.

Carly called the EMS and talked to the dispatcher who answered, explaining her situation to him. He told her, "I wasn't the dispatcher on duty then, and the trip sheets are with the crew who are on call at the moment. You'll have to call the police; all the calls go through them. Just give them the information that you gave me, and I'm sure they'll be able to help. Good luck."

Carly had to ask someone for the number to the local precinct. The aide handed Carly the number, saying how bad she felt about the situation. Carly looked at her and said, "You know too? I really don't care what he did; all I want right now is to find his belongings."

The aide left and Carly began to shake. "Mom, don't let anyone see that this is getting to you. You hold your head up, you did nothing wrong, they did."

Carly got a hold of the police and again explained her situation. "Mrs. Stevenson, if you could hold on for just one moment, I'll pull that call up on my computer for you. Okay, here it is. Yes, we had a call to the Whispering Pines Motel at about seven a.m. Your husband, Brad Stevenson, was transported by ambulance to County General Hospital. Is there anything else that we can do for you?"

"Well, in fact, yes there is something else that you could help me with. I'm at the hospital and I don't know where his belongings are; his car, or his money. Do you know of any way that I could go about locating them?"

"Well, you would have to go to the motel and see if his things are there. If not, then you'd have to file a stolen property report so that we could start looking for those items. Is there anything else I can help you with?"

"No officer, you have helped me out more than you know, thank you very much." Carly hung up the phone, turned to Cassie, and said, "Come on honey, let's get the hell out of here. I need a pay phone, now!"

Carly explained everything to Cassie as they walked to the pay phone outside. Cassie was speechless. Carly picked up the phone and called Lindsey, "Lindsey, I need to talk to Dom, is he there?"

"No Carly, but I can call him on his cell phone. What's going on?"

"Honey, Brad has had a severe stroke; He was brought into the hospital by ambulance from the fucking Whispering Pines Motel in his underwear. Now, I need to try to find his clothes, money, and car; that's why I need Dom. I need him and Ken to go there and get his stuff."

Lindsey couldn't believe what she was hearing. "I can't believe my ears. Are you okay? Is Cassie with you?"

"Oh, yeah, she's here, listening to all the shit that's going on. I'll tell you what, I've just about had it. I'm embarrassed enough, but for her to have to hear all this just kills me. Wait a minute

Lindsey, I've just been paged to go to Brad's room. Don't have Dom do anything until I call you back."

With that, she hung up the phone. She and Cassie hurried back inside and up to Brad's room. They entered the room to find the nurse there holding Brad's clothes and shoes. "How did you get those?" Carly asked the nurse in wonder.

"Someone brought them in to the ER a few minutes ago. Also, his car has been brought in to the parking lot."

"Do you know who brought his things?"

"No, I'm sorry, I don't, but I was told that everything is all here."

The nurse left and Carly told Steve to take Cassie home, "She's been through enough for one day. Take her home and make sure Ann and the baby are okay. Cassie, fill your sister in on what's been going on and tell Mom and Jerry to get here as soon as possible. I just need a couple of minutes to clear my head. I'll be fine. You two get going, and kiss the kids for me."

Cassie and Steve left and Carly was finally alone with Brad. She sat down in the chair across the room, not wanting to even be near him, let alone touch him. She talked aloud to him even though she knew he couldn't understand a word that she was saying.

"How could you do this to me? If you didn't love me anymore then why didn't you just leave? Now what am I supposed to do? How am I going to clean up this mess? I was leaving you; I was over everything. Now what do I do? I can't even stand to look at you, yet I'm the one that has to pick up the pieces of your shattered brain, and try to put them back together again. I really wouldn't have cared if you had left me. It would have been easier than going through this."

She put her head in her hands and sobbed uncontrollably. No one outside of this room would see the pain and humiliation on her face, even Brad wouldn't see it; hell, he didn't even know who she was.

CHAPTER SEVENTEEN

The Secret Is Out

About three o'clock in the afternoon, the doctors started to come in and check on Brad. Carly had a lot of questions for them, the main one was, if Brad was going to live. While Doctor Matthews began to check on Brad, Carly asked, "Doctor, can you tell me exactly what is wrong with him and how bad is he?"

Dr. Matthews looked up and asked, "May I ask you who you are?"

"I'm sorry. I should have introduced myself; I'm Brad's wife. My name is Carly Stevenson."

Dr. Matthews's reaction to her introduction was odd; he looked at her very strangely. "Mrs. Stevenson, Brad's not doing too well at all. He has had a severe stroke on the left side of his brain. That part controls the right side of his body plus comprehension, speech, and memory." The doctor demonstrated just what that meant. He lifted Brad's right leg and it fell right back onto the bed. The same thing happened when he lifted Brad's right arm. He asked Brad his name and got no response; he asked him who Carly was, and still no response. "We did a CT scan earlier and the pictures all showed major damage. There may be brain swelling as well, so we'll have to wait and watch him for the next several days. There's no point in straining him, he needs his rest."

Carly was in a daze, the words SEVERE kept echoing through her mind, "What are all the machines for?"

"Well, one is a heparin drip; a blood thinner to try and prevent another stroke. The other is glucose, to re-hydrate him, we think the stroke affected his throat, we are not sure if he can swallow without choking. The third is antivant, his alcohol level was very high when he came in and we didn't want him to go through withdrawal. The oxygen is for his lungs; he's very congested, probably from heavy smoking. The heart monitor is just in case there are heart problems. He is also catheterized, because he has no bladder control; he'll be diapered in a few days.

Well, Mrs. Stevenson, I hope I've given you what you're looking for as far as Brad's condition is concerned. Tomorrow we'll know more. From here on in, we just have to take it one day at a time."

Well, if Carly wanted information, she got it, medical information, that is. She was too exhausted, however, to think about digging into all the other messes that lay ahead. The doctor turned to go, leaving her wondering where she was going to get the strength to face the days ahead. Just as the doctor walked out the door, Jerry and Denise walked in.

Denise was visibly shaken. It was very difficult to see her so upset, she was in ill health, and Carly was worried. Jerry helped Denise to a chair and got her a glass of water. Neither one of them knew the circumstances that surrounded his stroke. After explaining only the essentials to Denise, Carly pulled Jerry into the hall and explained to him the other events of the morning.

Jerry looked at Carly and said to her, "My God Carly, you said that Brad was heading for a heart attack or stroke, and you were right. Look at him. Now you have to contend with this stupid affair of his. I wish that you had left in November when you wanted to. What are you going to do now?"

"Beats the shit out of me, but I'm not taking this lying down. There are too many unanswered questions, and I'm going to get those answers no matter what.

Jerry, Mom doesn't need to be here for all of this or for long. Please take her home and don't tell her anything about the mess Brad's in. I don't want her to get more upset than she already is. There's nothing more you can do here, and you have a long ride

home. I'll walk you out; I need a smoke and a cup of coffee myself."
Denise kissed Brad on the cheek after they returned and explained
they were leaving. She started to cry all over again and that's when
they knew it was time for all of them to go.

Going outside was a good idea, the sun was bright, and the
breeze mild and warm. *If she could just clear her head enough to get a
game plan together. Too many questions, not enough answers. There
were answers out there; it was just a matter of asking the right questions
to right people. Phone calls had to be made. Jack, the insurance company,
and she had to call work. It looked as if she wouldn't be going back to
work for a long time, if ever. Once again, her needs were being pushed
aside for Brad.*

The nurse was in with Brad as Carly came back into the room.
Brad looked anxious; somewhere in his mind, he was realizing that
something was very wrong. "Mrs. Stevenson, you should go home,
I'm going to sedate Brad for the night and the doctor's are done
with their rounds. You look exhausted and tomorrow will be a
busy day for you."

"You know, I think you're right. I haven't eaten and I have a lot
of phone calls to make. Brad's Dad lives in California and he needs
to be told. We live just five minutes away from here, so if you need
me, please call. I can be here quickly."

"He'll be fine. You're the one that needs to get some rest, I'm
sure that you're emotionally drained by now."

Her thoughtfulness moved Carly, finally someone who had
thought about her. She called Dom and arranged for him and Ken
to get Brad's car. Thank God, they would drive his car; the thought
of her getting into it made her sick to her stomach. The nurse was
preparing Brad for the night as Carly left. Dom and Ken met
Carly by the front door; the look on both their faces was one of
total bewilderment.

"What the hell's going on Carly?" Ken asked staring into Carly's
eyes. "Is he going to be alright?"

"I have no idea, but it's one fucked up mess and I'm stuck
right in middle of it."

Dom was quiet, as if he was thinking hard about something.

Carly let it go; she just wanted to get the hell out of there. As she drove home, all the emotions that she had kept bottled up inside all day finally came to a climax. Tears began to stream uncontrollably down her face, flowing nonstop as she sobbed out loud, "How could you do this to me, to the girls, to the whole family? You were so selfish, so self-centered, now we all have to pay the price for what you have done. If only I would have left in November, but now the whirlwind has sucked me down, again. Oh, why didn't I just leave? What the fuck was my problem? Damn you Brad, damn your girlfriend, damn you both!"

* * *

Marnie was going crazy; she couldn't call the hospital to check on Brad. What if Carly was there? She was sure that the word had spread through the hospital about what had happened, and she couldn't take the chance of stirring up any more trouble. Tonight she was scheduled to work from eleven to seven. No matter what, she was determined to see Brad and find out for herself what the hell was going on.

The hospital was in abuzz with the day's events. It was like a small community; news traveled fast. As Marnie entered the locker room, Cally, one of her friends, grabbed her by the shoulders, "What the hell happened? I just heard about you and Brad. What were you thinking?"

"Cally, I love him and I'm so worried, I don't know what I'm going to do."

"Look honey, you'd better think long and hard about this. Do you want this kind of responsibility? Even if he is divorced, you're young and can't take care of him forever; he's ten years older than you."

"Cally, he's not divorced, he's still married."

"Oh, that's just great! How could you get involved with a married man? You're going to be in deep shit if his wife finds out who you are. Where were your brains?"

"I don't know. I don't know anything, except that the man I love is lying helpless upstairs, and I have to go to him."

"Well, you'd better be careful. News travels fast around here and you could lose your job over this if the wrong people get wind of what's going on."

"Cally, I don't give a shit about my job right now. All I can think about is Brad!"

Marnie put on her uniform and hurried to go see Brad. She walked passed his room to make sure that no one was in there. As she entered his room her knees almost buckled, "Oh God! Brad, you look worse than this morning." She leaned over him and talked close into his ear. "It's me, honey, Marnie. Brad, please give me a sign that you know who I am, please try hard." Tears were pouring down her face; she so desperately wanted just a simple response. She reached down and held him close to her.

He was so weak, so frail; it ripped her heart apart. "Please Brad, come back to me. I love you so much, I need you to be with me." If only he could give her some kind of sign that he knew her, but there was no response. She was crushed. Kissing Brad on the forehead, she whispered, "I'll be back everyday, I'll always be here for you, soon you'll know me and remember what we had. You'll see honey, everything will be just the way it was. It has to be."

*   *   *

Carly pulled into the driveway followed by Dom and Ken. Dom was still very quiet. Carly just attributed it to the fact that he and Brad were very close and that he was worried. "If you need anything," Ken said to Carly, "just call me or Mandy, we'll help you with anything you need."

"Thanks Ken, but I'll be fine. I just need to eat something and call Brad's Dad, then try to get some rest."

"Well, if you need anything, just give us holler."

As soon as Carly closed the door, she fell apart. "What the hell am I going to do now?" she said out loud as she slid down to the floor, kneeling and praying for an answer to come down and save her.

Carly went to the kitchen to make a drink. Her whole body was numb. She made a drink and thought of how grateful she was for the help Ken and Dom gave her. Support and love from good friends who understood her pain was just what she needed.

But why was Dom so quiet? Normally he'd be very inquisitive, asking questions and searching for information, but not a word was said. Just then the doorbell rang; it was Dom. "Hi, Carly, can I come in?"

"Sure Dom. I was making myself a drink, can I get you one?"

"No, but I'll have a beer. We need to talk."

Dom and Carly moved into the living room. Dom couldn't hide the pain of guilt that was on his face. The burden that he had been carrying in his heart was about to be revealed. "I have something I have to get off my chest." He could hardly look at Carly. "I can't keep this from you anymore. I knew Brad was having an affair. I don't know all the details, but while you were in India he was acting strange. He wouldn't come over and hang out. He'd get dressed, leave, and not come home 'till morning."

Carly's face turned ashen white. "Why didn't you tell me, why didn't you at least give me a heads up? How could you not say anything?"

"Hey, I really didn't have anything to say until April. Every time I asked him what was going on, he'd change the subject, but last month he told me he met someone. That's all he said. I know I should have come to you, but I was hoping he'd come to his senses and end it. I really tried to tell him what he was doing was wrong, but he just laughed and told me I was jealous.

I'm so sorry all of this happened. He's my best friend and now he has lost everything. I really don't know how long things have been going on. Maybe he just met her. I know that he has been running around for a while; but with her, I don't know. The only person that can answer that is Brad, and he can't answer anything now. I'm so sorry Carly. Maybe he'd be okay if I would have come to you." The pain on Dom's face broke Carly's heart. How hard it must have been, torn between being Brad's best friend and telling her what was going on.

"Dom, you have no reason to feel guilty. You were between loyalties to Brad and our friendship. Trying to stop Brad from self-destruction would have been like stopping a runaway train. You could have never stopped him." Dom put his arms around Carly.

"Whatever you need just call, Lindsey and I will be there for the both of you." Dom left and Carly closed the door.

"What the hell am I going to do now?" She cried aloud. She prayed for answers from above. Another drink to calm her nerves, another cigarette and then call Jack.

Carly made herself a drink, lit a cigarette, then dialed Jack's phone number. Telling him wouldn't be easy. Even though they weren't that close, Brad was still his only child. "Jack? Hi, it's Carly. I've got some bad news to tell you. Brad is in the hospital; he's had a stroke. He's stable, but he's in pretty bad shape. The doctors will be in tomorrow and I should have more information by then." Carly left out all the gory details, and just stuck strictly to his medical condition. *Why tell him everything now? she thought. It wouldn't solve anything.* She could hear Jack sobbing.

It was very hard to hear that his only child had just had a stroke and may never recover. "Carly, don't call me. I'll call you around ten o'clock every night. Come home first, get something to eat, and then we can talk. You can fill me in every night on his progress. But, if there is a crisis, call me immediately."

"Thanks, Dad, and don't worry, he's in good hands at County General. After all, he works there. They'll take special care of him because he's an employee."

"True, that makes me feel a little better. Now you take care of yourself and I'll call you tomorrow."

As Carly hung up the phone, her thoughts turned towards the other woman. Who was she, how long had this been going on, and where did he meet her? The answers to these questions would all come in time. She knew that the answers would not make her happy. Of course, she hadn't been happy for a while and wasn't going to for a very long time, if ever.

CHAPTER EIGHTEEN

Who **are** you?

Marnie worked her shift in a daze. She couldn't think clearly; her mind was always on Brad. He had to recover, he just had to. Their life together depended on it. How could she face a life without him? She had waited so long to fall in love with the right man, and now a stroke may have taken that away from her. She couldn't even let herself think that way. He would get better; he had to.

Marnie went to check on his progress, but she just couldn't bring herself to pick up his chart and read it. That would have drawn too much attention, so she asked Cally to keep her updated on his progress.

"Marnie, Brad's condition is very severe. His stroke hit his left side of his brain, which controls his speech and memory. Full recovery from that type of stroke is nearly impossible. Please think this through, girl. You're young; you have your whole life ahead of you. Don't tie yourself up taking care of an invalid. I know you love him, but think damnit, he's got a family! Let them deal with this and get out while you still can."

"Cally, you don't understand. If there's the slightest chance that he will recover and remember me and what we had together, I have to take that chance and wait for as long as I can. I love him and I just can't turn off my feelings. He's all I can think about!"

The corridors of the hospital were quiet on the night shift. Brad and Marnie used to steal away into an empty room for a kiss when no one was around. They had even made love in one of the closed down units. Now as she walked the halls, she felt so alone. The pain ripped at her heart. Would she ever see Brad walk down the hall again? Would he ever be able to surprise her with a kiss and a hug? *He'll come back to me. He has to,* she thought to herself. Positive thoughts were what kept her going.

*   *   *

Carly awoke from a restless night's sleep. Not wanting to face the day ahead of her, she tossed and turned in bed. She twisted her wedding ring around and around on her finger. It meant nothing to her now, just pain, thoughts of unfulfilled dreams, and broken vows. The phone rang and Carly jumped up to answer it, thinking that it might be the hospital. It was Ann.

"Mom, are you okay? Cassie told me everything. What the hell are you going to do?"

"Ann, I don't have the slightest idea. Right now my head feels like it's going to explode. I can't focus on anything."

"Well, if you want my opinion, after what he has done to you, I would let his girlfriend figure out what to do with him. This isn't the first time that he's hurt you. It's time for you to get on with your own life. Believe me; no one would blame you if you just walked away. You have a great job, and you can live your life without all the hassle."

Ann was making a lot of sense, but she just didn't understand. If Brad's mind were functional, she could leave and never look back. Until she knew what the prognosis was going to be, she couldn't make any rash decisions. "Ann, I know what you are saying, and you're probably right. But until I can think clearly, I'm not making any decisions."

"Okay, Mom, I just want you to know that whatever you decide, I'll be there for you."

"Thanks honey, I love you and I know you mean well, but this has to be my decision and mine alone."

"Love you too, Mom. Call me when you have more news."

Carly got up and dressed and left for the hospital. If only her insides would stop shaking, she might actually be able to focus. As she walked into the hospital, Carly felt the hospital walls closing in, smothering the life right out of her. She took a deep breath and boarded the elevator, a ride that she would take many more times before this was all over. Steve had already dropped Cassie off and she waited for Carly upstairs.

"Cassie you should be at work. I don't want you to get into trouble by taking off. I can handle this myself."

"Nothing to worry about Mom, you need someone here with you. I have some sick days coming, and after yesterday, you're not going through this alone. If everything is alright, I'll go back to work next week."

"Thanks honey, I really could use someone. I'm glad you're here with me. Have any of the doctors come in while you've been here?"

"I just got here five minutes ago, and no one has been in yet."

Just then, the inhalation therapist came in and gave Brad his breathing treatment. Brad showed no sign of knowing him, even though they had worked together for years.

Carly asked the therapist, "Have the doctors started their rounds yet? Have I missed anyone?"

"The doctors are working their way up the hall now. They should be in shortly."

After the therapist was finished, Carly went over to the side of the bed and talked to Brad. "Brad, it's me, Carly. Can you hear me? Do you know who I am?" Brad gave Carly a blank frightened stare. He looked like a scared little child who was unable to talk.

"Mom, I tried when I first came in, but I got the same reaction. Nothing."

"This isn't good. I was hoping for some kind of response today."

Just then, Dr. Morrison walked in. Carly had never met her before, but recognized her name from the chart on the door. The doctor checked Brad's eyes and read his chart from the night before.

"Can you tell me how Brad is doing? I am very concerned about his condition. Are there any changes that we should know about?" Carly asked.

"Not really. We are in a watch and wait situation. Our main concern right now is to stabilize his vitals and wait for the brain swelling to go down."

Cassie looked at the doctor and asked, "Will he ever fully recover, or is his condition permanent?"

"Well, the CT scan showed a massive stroke. We'll get a better picture of the situation from the MRI that we'll perform on Brad in a few days. We want him to rest before we do more tests."

Carly asked, "Will he have to be catheterized permanently?"

"No, we'll diaper him tomorrow. We just wanted to measure his fluid out-put to make sure that his kidneys were working. As I said, we are in a watch and wait situation."

The nurse came into the room and asked Carly to come with her to the nurse's station to accept a phone call. It was Denise. Carly had told her yesterday to call the nurse's station instead of Brad's room, in case no one was in the room to answer the phone. Carly excused herself and left Dr. Morrison and Cassie alone.

Dr. Morrison turned to Cassie and asked, "I'm sorry I have to ask this, but who is that woman?"

"What do you mean, 'who is that woman?' That's his wife and my mother."

"I'm very sorry to have asked that, but I was under the impression that Brad was divorced and that his new wife had admitted him to the hospital."

"There is no new wife. They have been married for thirty years and never divorced. I wish everyone in this place would get the facts straight."

Carly re-entered the room while the doctor said goodbye and left. Cassie was in tears, "Cassie, what's wrong? Why are you crying? What happened while I was on the phone?"

"Mom, are these people crazy, or is it just me? No one here knows who the hell you are! What has Dad been telling everyone?"

It finally dawned on her. Brad must have told them that they had gotten a divorce following their separation. He never told them that they had reconciled. No wonder they had no idea who she was. They thought that he had a new wife all along. What a creative liar he was. "Don't worry, honey. Before this is over, they'll all know who the real Mrs. Stevenson is."

Cassie and Carly left for lunch while Brad was sleeping. Carly had to get out of there; she needed a cigarette and a drink. "Cassie, after lunch why don't you leave. There's nothing more that you can do here, and the kids need you at home." Carly didn't want her getting any more upset then she already was.

"Mom, you're right, I'll go; but you'd better watch your back, something's not right here. I can't put my finger on it but something's up and it's not good."

"I agree Cassie, I'll be careful. I'm going to get to the bottom of this. There's got to be someone who knows what's going on and I'll find them."

After lunch, Cassie left to go home as Carly headed to The Club. It was the place that she and Brad had gone to for years and they had a lot of friends there. She was hoping that maybe Brad had told someone something, anything, about what was going on. She hadn't been there for months, but maybe Brad had gone there, gotten drunk, and spilled his guts to one of the guys. It was a long shot, but she may as well try, she had nothing else to lose. The Club was pretty empty, it was after lunch, and everyone had already gone back to work.

Carol, the owner, came over to Carly as she walked in, "Well, where the hell have you been keeping yourself? It's been months since you've been in to see me. What's going on?"

Carol looked stunned as Carly briefly filled her in on what had been happening the last few days, "Carol, can you tell me anything that could help me figure out what's been happening? I'm at my wits end."

"Honey, you could have knocked me over with a feather. You know the guys that come in here don't tell me anything. But, I did overhear Pete and Ted talking about Brad a couple of days ago.

I kind of thought that you and Brad were having problems when he kept coming in here without you. I'd ask him where you were and he'd just say that you were working. The last couple of times he was here, he wouldn't even look my way, and he was drinking a lot, even for him. I heard the guys talking about him and some nurse at the hospital. Now I didn't catch everything, but I gathered it had been going on for a couple of months, at the least."

Carly grabbed the first chair she could and sat down. Carol got her a drink and sat down next to her. "Christ Carol, that means she probably works at the hospital. I might have passed her in the halls, she may even be one of the nurses taking care of him. No wonder all kinds of strange shit has been happening there. It's all starting to make sense."

"Look, Honey, it sounds like you'd better think long and hard about what your next move is going to be. I wish I could've told you this sooner, but you haven't been in, and I didn't know how to get in touch with you."

"Carol did you catch a name, what she looks like, anything that could help me?"

"No, Carly. I've told you everything I heard. Have you looked through his wallet or his car? You know men, they keep their lives in their wallets and their glove compartments."

"Carol, you're a genius! I never even thought about looking there. I haven't been able to even look at his car, let alone search it. I have to go back to the hospital now, but when I get back home I'm going to start looking around for clues."

They hugged each other and said good-bye. Carly left The Club on a mission. She had to watch her back now. Everyone there must know what's been going on, and they would take care of their own; she was the outsider. Maybe tonight her search would give her a place to start.

CHAPTER NINETEEN

Carly Now Calls the Shots

Marnie looked in the mirror, "God you look like crap," she said aloud. "You've got to pull yourself together and stop crying," but she couldn't. Every time she thought about Brad lying in that hospital bed all alone, it broke her heart. Marnie combed her hair, and left early to go see him, she had gotten him flowers. *Everyone else in the hospital had already dropped in to see him. I'll just take the flowers in and not leave a card, no one would know who they were from*, she thought. She was determined to see Brad.

When she got to the locker room to change her clothes, Cally met her at the door. "Marnie, you'd better be careful. Brad's wife and daughter have been in and out all day and his wife looks mighty upset. I have a feeling that she knows that something's not right and you know, it's not going to take her long to figure out that he's been seeing someone here."

"I know Cally, but I've got to get in to see him. I won't wear my nametag and I'll just take a few minutes. Please Cally, don't try and stop me." Marnie had already made up her mind and nothing was going to stop her from seeing Brad.

"Well, at least let me go with you and stand watch by the door."

"Thanks Cally, I promise to be quick. I just have to hold his hand, kiss him and tell him that I love him."

"Marnie, you know that I'm totally against this relationship, but I love you, girl; and if I can't stop you, at least I can try to protect you."

Marnie had never seen Carly, but she had a feeling that she would recognize her. A confrontation in the hospital was the last thing either one of them needed, especially if her daughters were with her; that would be ugly.

If only all this hadn't happened. For the first time in two years, Marnie had actually felt like she had a real shot at happiness. Now she didn't have any idea of what the future held. Deep in her heart, she knew that Brad would have left Carly to be with her, then both of their lives would have been perfect.

As they got to his room, Marnie was relieved, "Good, there's no one in there with Brad, they must have left for awhile. Cally, you stand by the door; I'm going in to see Brad."

Cally stood outside the door feeling very uncomfortable. She hated being in the middle of this, but she wanted to help Marnie, even though she was against the whole situation.

Marnie immediately went over to Brad. She kissed him on the lips and leaned over to hold his hand. "Honey, Brad, it's me, Marnie. I'm here, sweetheart. I've brought you flowers. I love you so much, can you let me know if you recognize me?" Brad looked over at Marnie, but his blank stare sent a chill up her spine.

"Oh God, Brad, try to say something, anything. I can't stand that I can't reach you. Please, Brad. I love you so much, please try harder." Marnie was crying and shaking all over. Brad just looked at her as if she wasn't even there.

Cally leaned in to the room, "Marnie, come on, they may come back at any time. Please, let's go."

"Okay, I'm coming." Marnie hugged Brad and kissed him one more time before she said good-bye. "I'll be back tomorrow darling, you'll see. You'll be better, trust me." Marnie left the room feeling emotionally drained, every fiber of her being, ached.

"Cally, I'm going to see Brad tomorrow, too; I know if I see him every day, he'll remember who I am. Please Cally, you have to help me."

"Okay Marnie, I'll help you, but you better be extremely careful."

*   *   *

Carly got back to the hospital later then usual. Brad was still asleep, but restless. Carly noticed the flowers on the windowsill. She went over to read the card and couldn't find one. *Now I just wonder who brought these to you, Brad,* she thought to herself. *Must have been some naive little bitch who thinks he's just going to jump right out of bed and pick up where they left off.* She almost laughed aloud at the stupidity of it all. There he was, with IV's, monitors, oxygen, and a catheter, he doesn't even know his elbow from his ear, and she thought he was going to remember her, how foolish. She almost felt sorry for her, that is, if she didn't hate her with every cell of her body.

The love, attention, and affection Carly so desperately needed and wanted went all to her instead. Carly had even tried to buy his love, but he had given it all to the 'other woman' freely and willingly. Why was it that she was thrown out like yesterday's trash, and this woman was treated with such love and care? She would always hate them both; they shared the love that she had wanted all her life.

Carly couldn't change what had happened, but she could change others' perception of her. She made up her mind that from that moment on that she would be the one calling the shots. She had finally gotten a handle on how to play the game. Come what may, no one would look at her as a poor, pathetic, tossed-aside wife. Carly wanted everyone to ask themselves, "Why would Brad ever cheat on her? He must have been crazy to dump someone like her."

The next morning, her business suit came out of the closet. If she had to be on display in the hospital everyday, then she was going to give them something to look at. From her position as a personal assistant, power dressing was something that she knew about all too well. Representing her boss at functions meant dressing the part, and she had done that very well. From now on, she would be in charge, so they'd all better get the hell out of her way.

The neurologists met with Carly in the lounge. "Mrs. Stevenson, Brad's condition is critical. The next seventy-two hours will tell us what to expect. He hasn't improved very much at all. As you have observed, he still has no use of his right arm or any movement in his right leg. As far as comprehension, the tests reveal limited to no comprehension. We're sure his short-term memory is completely gone, probably from the last two years, and chunks of his long-term memory are gone as well. That's not to say that some of it might not come back in time. Yet, it will be a long drawn out process to try and retrieve what it is that he has left, and to try and train the living cells of the brain that are still active."

"Will the therapy help him regain the use of his right side and help him to talk?" Carly felt weak in the knees and had to sit down.

"Mrs. Stevenson, can I get you a glass of water?" Dr. Collins was afraid that Carly might faint.

"No, I'm alright, thanks. It's just a lot of information to digest at one time."

"Well, five years ago with a stroke victim as bad as Brad, we would never have recommended therapy. But now, with intense work, we've found that therapy, while not a cure, can still improve the quality of life for the victim and family. We do give the advice though, to be prepared that if things don't improve with Brad. The idea of moving him to a nursing home may still be necessary, and even if things do get a lot better, we would suggest a one-floor dwelling. He won't be able to manipulate steps for quite awhile, if ever."

"Now, wait a minute. It's only been a few days since the stroke, are you getting ready to discharge him?" Carly had no intention of moving and changing her life around any more then it had already changed.

"Oh, heavens, no. We just want you to be aware of these things so that when we do discharge Brad, you won't be caught off guard."

"At this point, you can't tell me if Brad will even survive this stroke. If he does and can come home, I can be ready in three days but I'm not moving. If I have to, I'll get a stair lift or a portable facility and a hospital bed. Why don't you concentrate on making him well, and let me worry about how and where we're going to live."

Dr. Collins saw the determination in Carly's eyes, "Mrs. Stevenson, I'm very sorry if I upset you, but I'm required to tell you what may lie ahead."

"I'm sorry if I seem abrupt, I'm tired and I'm upset, but believe me, when the time comes, I'll make the right decisions. Just give me three to four days notice and things will be taken care of."

Dr. Collins left Carly in the lounge. She had a lot to think about, hell, she didn't even know if she would be taking him home. The thought of having to take care of him forever scared her to death and was infuriating as well. Why should she have to give up her life to take care of him? When he had a whole brain, he wanted to be with someone else other then her. She took her wedding vows seriously, but this seemed to go beyond what she had promised.

She decided to leave the hospital earlier than usual, her head was pounding, and there wasn't any room in her brain for one more medical term or one more decision that had to be made. Besides, Ann and the baby were coming in to see Brad tomorrow. It had taken a lot to convince Ann to see her father. Her mind had already been made up, never wanting to see him again after what he had done to Carly.

"Mom, I don't think I can stomach looking at him after what he's done to you. To be honest with you, I hope he rots in hell."

"Ann, he's still your father. You have to see for yourself what's going on here, then you can decide how you feel. I know that he's hurt you and I know that he's hurt me, but you need to see him the way he is now. We can bring Dakota in too, I already cleared that with the nurse. Seeing the baby might trigger something in him. Please say you'll come in with the baby, not for his sake maybe, but for yours." Carly knew that once Ann saw her father in the state that he was in, it would help her understand how complicated the whole situation was. Just as important, she would see how difficult deciding to leave Brad would be.

Instead of going home, Carly went to The Club. Dinner first, then enough drinks to dull the pain, even if only for a few hours. She sat down in a secluded corner not wanting to face anyone; she couldn't answer questions that she had no answers to. After dinner, she ordered one drink after the other. Slowly the tension was released from her neck, and a light fog wrapped around her like a blanket. She sat in the corner, in the dark, letting her brain go numb. When the music changed to love songs, Carly was overwhelmed with emotion.

She went over to Carol, her eyes filled with tears, "Please Carol, change the CD's to something else, you're killing me with these songs."

"Oh God, Carly I didn't even know you were here. I'll get Joey to change the music, you just sit back down and relax."

"You know what, don't bother. I need to go home and try to get some sleep. I think the drinks are hitting me, and I better stop now; I have to drive home."

"Honey, can I call you a cab? I don't want you to have a problem driving."

"No Carol, I'm fine, I'm not drunk, I'm just numb."

Instead of going straight home, Carly drove to the Whispering Pines Motel. She sat in her car in the parking lot. It was strange, she should have been crying, pounding the dashboard, or feeling something, but she was numb, just numb. All she could do was sit and stare at the rooms. Which room did he take her to? Did he hold her tightly and tell her that he loved her, was he happy to be with her?

Their life together wasn't what she had always hoped it would be, but she never thought that he would humiliate her by carrying on an affair with someone in the hospital. She shouldn't have ever had to face those people, especially with them knowing so much about her private life. If only he would have been man enough to ask for a divorce. That would have been painful, but at least she could have been free of the problems that she was faced with now.

There were no answers at the Whispering Pines Motel, only more questions. It was time to go home. A cold chill went over her as she drove home. She had been so close to freedom, why had that choice been taken away from her? Too tired to think, she went into the house and collapsed into her bed. She cried into her pillow, "Damn you, Brad! Why couldn't you love me the way you must have loved her? What did I do wrong?" She closed her eyes and cried herself to sleep.

CHAPTER TWENTY

Ann Now Understands

Marnie slipped into Brad's room before she left for home. "Just one more time today, I have to see him," she said to herself as she entered his room. She opened the door to find that the nurse was changing Brad's diaper.

"Marnie, what are you doing here so late?"

Evidently this nurse was one of the few people in the hospital that hadn't heard about her and Brad. "Oh, Brad and I have been friends for a long time. I just thought I'd pop in to see how he was doing." Her voice was shaking, and she was flushed; she wasn't expecting anyone to be in the room.

"Well, Marnie, he's not doing well tonight. He's very restless and agitated. Maybe you should stop in tomorrow during visiting hours."

"Sure, no problem, I'll stop in then."

As she left the room, her whole body was trembling. That was too close, she would have to be more careful. If only she could have kissed him though, and told him that she loved him. When he started to remember their life together, she wanted to be there to show him that she had been waiting patiently for him to recover; that she hadn't deserted him. "Tomorrow, darling. I'll see you then," she whispered at the door.

* * *

Carly laid in bed, her head thumping. The drinks she'd had the night before had put her to sleep, but the headache she had now was the payback for too much alcohol. She got up, took two aspirin, and stepped into a hot shower. The steam from the water filled the bathroom. She breathed in the vapors to clear her head; the hot water made her body tingle. It had been months since Brad and her had made love. Her body ached for the touch of a man.

She was still a vibrant sexual woman. If only she would have left Brad in November, maybe she could have found someone who would appreciate her for the woman that she was and give her the love that she craved. Now her future was as cloudy as the steam that surrounded her. She trembled at the thought of a life alone.

She took extra care in selecting her clothes; they had to exude authority and power. No one was going to take pity on her; on the contrary, from now on they would wonder why Brad ever treated her the way that he did. On her break in the afternoon, she would tear apart Brad's car. She was hoping to find a photo, a name, or some other clue as to who the mystery woman was.

Carly walked into the hospital with a newfound mind set. She carried herself like a woman on a mission, and it showed. The head nurse stopped Carly before she entered Brad's room, "Mrs. Stevenson, Brad's down in x-ray, he tried to pull himself out of bed, and fell to the floor last night. He bruised his hip and we need to make sure that he didn't break it."

Carly saw the bed being wheeled back into the room. Brad looked confused. "From now on, I want him restrained at night so that this doesn't happen again. Brad told me many times that the family can request restraints at night, and I'm requesting them. Bring me the papers and I'll sign them right now." The nurse brought her the forms to sign. That was all she needed was for Brad to break his hip along with all the other problems he already had.

"Also, our daughter is coming in to see her Dad and she is bringing her new baby for Brad to see. Maybe seeing the baby will trigger some kind of a response in his mind. I'll take full responsibility for bringing the baby into the hospital." Carly was not asking for permission anymore, she was telling everyone what she was going to do. The nurse was not happy, but told Carly to keep the baby covered to protect him from the germs, and not to stay too long.

"I'm well aware of the germs in this place and so is Ann, she used to work as a nursing assistant in a personal care home. We'll take extra care."

Ann arrived with Dakota and Carly's heart filled with joy. She was very apprehensive to see how Ann would react to seeing her father. Carly had prepared her for what she would see, but what she would feel in her heart, well, that was another story. Ann's cheeks flushed as she entered the room. The father that she had come to despise was lying in a hospital bed looking like a frightened little child. There is a fine line between love and hate and Ann now dangled from it. Her eyes filled with tears; emotionally she was not prepared to see her father that way. She hated him for what he had done to her mother, but to see him lying there helpless as a baby jumbled all of her emotions.

She leaned in close to Brad, "Dad, it's Ann, how are you doing? Come on, give me that crooked smile Mom told me about." As tears streamed down her face, she leaned in closer to Brad and kissed him on the cheek. Brad looked up at Ann and gave her that smile. "Mom, do you think he knows who I am?"

"I don't know, Honey. Why don't you ask him again?"

"Dad, do you know who I am?" Brad looked at her with that confused, blank stare. He tried to speak, but the words weren't understandable. "Oh God. Mom, this is bad, this is very bad."

Ann lifted Dakota out of the carrier and put the baby on Brad's chest. She placed Brad's left hand on the baby and helped him to stroke his back. Brad looked at Dakota, smiled, then closed his eyes and went to sleep, as if soothed to sleep by the feel of a baby. Ann put Dakota back in his carrier, and fell into the chair.

Carly went over to her and gave her a hug. "I love you, Honey.

I know this is hard for you, but you had to see for yourself exactly what I'm dealing with. It's not a black and white situation. I can't make any rash decisions right now."

Ann looked into Carly's eyes, as they both cried. "Mom, I don't know what tell you to do. Before I came in this room I was so sure that you should just walk away, now I can't even begin to think what must be going on in your heart and mind. I do know that whatever decision you make it has to be yours and yours alone. You have to live with whatever you decide; no one can help you. I'll stand by you whatever you do, just think long and hard before you make your final decision."

Ann packed up the baby and kissed Carly good-bye. Carly sat down in the chair next to Brad's bed. She took his hand in hers and looked long and hard at his face. He looked almost child like, lying there so innocent. She hated the man that had the stroke, but how could she hate the man lying in this bed? This man had no memory, couldn't talk, and had no concept of the pain he had inflicted on everyone, now or in the past. How do you separate the two Brad's, how do you hate one and pity the other? "Oh God, how do I find the strength to sort all of this out without losing my mind in the process?" As she spoke aloud, Brad opened his eyes and looked at her, he didn't know what she said but he smiled at her and tried to speak. She could not understand what he was trying to say.

Carly could see the frustration on his face, he was trying to figure out what was wrong, and he looked frightened. "Just rest Brad, don't try and talk. Once you've had some therapy you'll be able to say something, it's too soon to try and force yourself."

The speech therapist knocked on the door, "Hi, Speech Therapy. May I come in?"

"Sure, come on in. He was just trying to talk." Carly was glad to see her; maybe she could answer some questions.

"I'm going to test him with some pictures to check if he has any comprehension skills at all. This is just a preliminary test. It will give us an idea of what direction we need to go in concerning his treatment." The therapist held up two different pictures, one was a butterfly and the other a picture of a church. "Brad, please pick out the butterfly." The therapist lifted his hand and again said, "Brad, point to the butterfly." Brad lifted his finger and pointed to the church. She asked him again and he pointed to the church again. "Well, let's try some numbers? Can you point to the number two?" Brad looked long and hard and picked out the number two from three different numbers. "Well, that's wonderful Brad. Now you rest you've had enough work out for the first visit."

When Carly realized that she had been holding her breath, she finally took a deep breath, "What does all this mean?"

"Numbers are the last thing a stroke victim loses, so at least we know that there's still something left in his brain to work with. How much is left remains to be seen."

Carly knew that it was too soon to get any more information from the therapist at that time; she would just have to be patient.

"I'll be back in a few days and start his therapy."

Dr. Collins came in, as the therapist was about to leave. "Well, how's our patient doing today?"

"Brad did very well on recognizing numbers, but he had difficulty with the visual test. It's still too early to make a full prognosis; we'll know more when he's moved to the third floor in about three days." The therapist then left.

Dr. Collins did some of his own tests on Brad. "Brad, can you lift your right arm? Brad, lift your right arm for me please." Brad didn't respond to the doctor, he just looked confused. "Can you lift your left arm?" still nothing. "Brad try and lift your left leg." This time Brad tried to lift his leg. "That's good Brad, you tried to lift your leg. That's very good."

The doctor looked to Carly and said, "The concept of lift is there, he's just not processing the full command. In time, I think he may be able to learn some of the things that he lost in the stroke. But it will take many, many months of therapy, and even then I can't tell you how much he will get back. I can tell you, it probably won't be much."

"When will he be able to drink water and eat something? He's losing weight so fast," Carly was concerned that Brad was getting too weak.

"We'll know as soon as we do the barium swallow test to see if his throat muscles work. We can't take the chance of him aspirating into his lungs, he could develop pneumonia, and we can't have that happen."

"What if his throat is paralyzed, how will he eat?"

"We'll tube feed Brad through his stomach. If that happens, it will be permanent."

Carly's face turned ashen gray, "God, I need to sit down. Can you get me a glass of water? I feel a little woozy."

"I know that you have a lot to think about, but in three days we should know if Brad can swallow and what course of therapy that we're going to follow. Let's take one day at a time, keep an open mind, and hope for the best."

Carly looked over at Brad; "It's just all so overwhelming."

Dr. Collins told Carly, "We'll do our best to help Brad, but you take care of yourself. This is only the beginning and there's a long road ahead of both of you."

Dr. Collins left Carly with a lot to think about. Carly brushed the hair off Brad's forehead, adjusted his blanket and fluffed his pillow. "I'm leaving now Brad; I'll be back in the morning. Don't try to get out of bed again; your legs are too weak and you'll fall. Please try and understand what I'm telling you." His eyes were so empty. All she could do was hope that he understood something she said. Carly headed over to the nurse's station, "Please make sure Brad is restrained tonight, I don't want him to fall out of his bed again."

"Mrs. Stevenson, we'll do our best to make sure Brad is taken care of." Her tone was sharp, almost offensive.

"Look, I signed the proper papers. Please see that the orders are carried out," Carly told the nurse with her tone just as sharp.

Carly left the hospital quickly. *Get me the hell out of this place,* she thought to herself. Fresh air, a cigarette, a drink, and some peace and quiet, was exactly what she needed. Besides, she had a job to do. She needed to search Brad's car for anything that would help her identify the woman that he loved. It was about time for her to find out who she was, maybe tonight.

CHAPTER TWENTY-ONE

A Name?

It had been two days since Marnie had seen Brad; she could hardly wait to get to the hospital to check on how he was doing. She had no clue that his stroke had erased any trace of their affair. If she had known, she would have been devastated.

The phone rang and Marnie answered, "Hi Marnie, it's your brother Bill, I'm so glad I caught you at home."

"You're lucky, I was just about to walk out the door. What's up?" Bill never called on a weekday and never this late.

"Mom's in the hospital. She's had a heart attack, it's pretty serious."

Marnie gasps, "When did it happen, where did it happen? Bill tell me everything."

"Marnie, can you please make arrangements to get down here? She needs by-pass surgery and I'm the only one here since Dad died last year. I don't want to go through this by myself, Marnie. I need you to get here as soon as possible. The operation is in four days; they have to stabilize her first."

Oh God, how could she leave now, what about Brad? "Can you give me three days? I'll put in for a leave of absence and clear up some things here."

"Okay, but try and get here as quickly as possible."

"Bill, I'll call in the morning with my flight time and number. Don't worry, I'll be there."

"What the hell else can happen?" she yelled aloud, after she hung up the phone.

She left for work quickly; she had to talk to Cally. She'd have to be her eyes and ears while she was gone. Cally and Marnie met in the locker room. "You'll have to help me, Cally. I have to leave for Florida in three days. My mother is having by-pass surgery and my brother Bill needs me to come down to Florida for support."

"Christ Marnie, that's terrible. What the hell else can happen to you? What do you want me to do while you're gone?"

"I'll call you every night to find out about Brad. I want you to visit him everyday and tell him that I love him and I'll be back to be with him soon."

"Look, Marnie, I'll check on him for you, but I'm not getting in the middle of this. He can't comprehend anything right now. Be patient, it's going to take a long time for him to regain even a small part of his memory. He won't even know you're gone."

"Cally, please, please, do this for me. I don't want to waste any opportunity to help him remember me and how much I love him." Marnie was sobbing. How could she leave him now, but how could she not be with her mother? Her heart was being torn to shreds.

"Marnie, I'll do what I can, but I'm not getting into trouble over this. I'm not making any promises."

"Alright Cally, I understand, I'll appreciate anything you can do for me." Marnie made her way to Brad's room. She stood in the doorway wanting to scoop him up and carry him home to be with her, but she realized that that was impossible. She entered the room and sat down on the bed next to Brad. She lifted his chin and kissed him softly on the lips. "Darling, I have to leave for a little while, but I'll be back as quickly as possible. The doctors will take good care of you while I'm gone. Maybe when I get back, some of your memory will have started to return and we can make plans to be together again. I'll be in tomorrow and I'll bring you something to remember me by while I'm away. Just try and remember that I love you. I need you to remember that I love you, and that you love me, and that we've planned to spend the rest of our lives together."

She kissed Brad again, her tears landing on Brad's cheek. He looked up at her, but didn't seem to understand what was going on. "I'll be back as quickly as possible, I love you." Marnie was crying so hard that she could barely breathe. Her precious Brad; how could she leave him now? But she knew she had no choice.

Carly left the hospital hell bent on putting the pieces of this puzzle together. If only she could find something; a name, a picture, anything that would help her to make sense of this senseless situation. As she pulled into the driveway, her heart was pounding wildly in her chest.

"I'm going to find something in his car if it kills me. I know Brad well enough to know that he must have left a clue somewhere. His car is the only place that he could have possibly hidden anything," she said aloud as she fumbled through her purse looking for Brad's spare keys.

As soon as she unlocked Brad's car, she began to look through his glove compartment. Registration papers, maintenance reports, sunglasses, but nothing else. She turned her search to the back of the car. Lying on the floor was a jacket; underneath the jacket was a small box. Her heart seemed to thump even faster. Could this be where he kept his secrets?

Her hands trembled as she opened up the box. Inside were letters, small little gifts, schedules stapled together. A hidden life laid bare right in her hands. Shuffling through the letters scented with perfume was heart wrenching for Carly. How could he have done this to her, how could he have been so cruel and heartless? As she opened one of the letters, her stomach turned to ice. The words burned through her soul. She read aloud,

"My Dearest darling, How can I tell you what last night meant to me? Your body so hot and firm, your lips so sweet. Our lovemaking is still so fresh in my mind. You please me in ways you don't even know. I can still feel you inside of me."

Carly dropped the letter to the floor. She could picture them together making love, wrapped in each other's arms, and she felt sick to her stomach. Maybe in the scheme of life, having a cheating husband was low on the scale of trauma in some people's minds, but to Carly it was the end of her life. Not only was she betrayed, but also now, she was left to clean up the messes that she didn't even cause. Now she was the one who remained to face a future that was full of uncertainty and loneliness.

By now, the tears were blinding her eyes. "Okay Carly," she said to herself, "let's find out the name of this person who loved your husband so much." She flipped to the end of the letter and read.

> *I love you Brad so much, from the depths of my soul. Now and forever, I'll always love you. With every breath I take, you are the beat of my heart.*
> *I love you Brad. I'll always love you.*
> *Forever and always*
>
> *Marnie*

Finally a name, but Marnie who? She sifted through the rest of the notes and papers and still no last name. Now what? She lit a cigarette and tried to compose herself, she had to think. She picked up the schedules that were stapled together; maybe her last name was on the schedule. When she looked closer, she found no name just little hearts next to the days that they were to meet. How sweet. Carly wasn't getting the answers that she had hoped to find.

Wait a minute, she thought, *if she brought him to the hospital, she had to have signed him in, her name would be on the admission papers.* In the morning she would check with Jan in the staffing office, maybe she could help her get a copy of the admission forms. Carly had never met Jan; she had just talked to her on the phone whenever she called Brad to come into work for extra hours.

As a matter of fact, she must have been the one that called Brad into work that night. Yet, Brad didn't go to work, so it couldn't have been Jan, it had to have been *her.* She must have wanted to make sure Brad kept his date with her and when Carly answered the phone, she pretended to be the staffing office. How many times had she called him pretending to be the staffing office? All this time, Carly thought that Brad had been working overtime, when really, he was with *her*. No wonder he was broke, he wasn't making any extra money, he was making love to *her*. Just to be sure, she would check with Jan in the morning to see if someone from the staffing office called that night. All these thoughts lingered in her head as she tried in vain to sleep.

The night before had drained the life out of Carly. Reading the love letters from Marnie to Brad, seeing with her own two eyes the words that made Brad's blood boil with lust, made her toss and turn all night. The words in those letters may have filled Brad's body with fire, but they burned a hole through Carly's heart. She pulled herself out of bed and got ready to face her day at the hospital once again.

Not knowing what or who she would find when she got there sent shivers down her spine. Would Brad be worse? Would she find out Marnie's last name, will she pass her in the hall not even knowing who it was? If Jan didn't call Brad into work, that meant Brad knew he was going to be with Marnie that night. That's why he said he wouldn't get fired going to work drunk, he knew he wasn't going to work. If only she could turn back the hands of time and erase all of the ugliness, but she couldn't. So instead, it was time to get to the business at hand and find the answers to all her questions.

Carly opened the door to the staffing office, "Excuse me, may I please speak with Jan?"

"Hi I'm Jan, may I help you?"

"I hope so. I'm Carly Stevenson, my husband Brad works here. I need to ask you a few questions."

"Okay."

"First, did the staffing office call Bard into work on the 29th?"

"Umm, let me check our log book, but I don't think so, we were fully staffed that night as I recall. Ah, here it is. Nope, no one was called into work that night. We had our normal shift working and Brad was off that night."

Carly's suspicions were correct; Marnie did call to make sure that Brad kept their date. "Second question."

"Yes?"

"I need to know who signed Brad into the ER that next morning. I was never called by the hospital and I need to find out who's signature is on the admissions forms."

"Carly I can't help you with that information. You'll have to go to patient records and see if they will give you that information. Or you could ask the nurse to see the chart."

"Thanks Jan, you've been very helpful." If Marnie signed her name to the admissions forms, Carly would have the answers she needed. How did she sign it, though, as a friend or as a wife? If she'd signed him in as his wife, that was fraud. Before she asked any more questions, maybe she'd better talk to her attorney.

Carly entered Brad's room to find they had sat him in a chair. "Well, look at you sitting up in a chair all by yourself!" He was strapped in the chair so he wouldn't fall out, but at least he wasn't lying in bed. It was very hard to be upbeat and perky when her life was crashing down around her. Yet, what good would it serve her or Brad to be hateful to a man that in all reality had no memory of what had happened to him or Carly.

The nurse on duty came into the room to get Brad back into bed. He was still on IV's, monitors, and oxygen, so getting him back into bed wasn't easy. Carly helped the nurse; he was so frail and weak that moving him was very difficult. "How long has he been sitting up in the chair?" Carly asked the nurse.

"Oh, about twenty minutes. We're trying to get him up so he can gain strength in his legs. But he's still very unstable and has to be watched very closely. He does try to help himself, so that's a good sign."

"How's his speech?"

"Not good. He still can't say anything that can be understood, and he still doesn't follow commands. But it is still very early, give it time."

Carly made sure Brad was settled in bed then followed the nurse out of the room. "Please make sure Brad gets a bed bath at some point today, and call me if there is any change. I have to leave early today, but I'll be back early in the morning."

The nurse wrote down Carly's phone number and told her that she'd call if there was a problem. Carly went back into Brad's room, checked to make sure he was settled; he was sleeping so she left. It was time to call her boss and tell her that she had to take an extended leave of absence. There was no chance that she could go back to work any time soon, if ever, so it was time to let her find a replacement. The job of her dreams was just another thing that Brad and Marnie had stolen from her.

Carly had to call Jack and give him the information that she had gotten from the doctor over the past few days. There was really nothing much to add to what he already knew, but at least he would know that there was no real change. After all the phone calls, after all the tears, Carly took a hot bath, drank a bottle of wine, and fell into bed. She was too numb to think, just drunk enough to sleep.

CHAPTER TWENTY-TWO

A Little Token of Love

Marnie had taken great care in picking out the perfect gift to leave for Brad. Something that hopefully no one would notice and Brad would somehow know it was from her. She had already asked Cally if giving Brad an earring was permitted. She checked the chart and told her there was no reason why he couldn't have it. All of Brad's jewelry was removed when he had arrived in the ER and, as Marnie noticed, had not been put back on. She had bought a small gold ball stud, and tonight she would leave it with Brad. Hopefully, he would reach up with his left hand, touch it, and think of her.

Brad was asleep when Marnie went into his room. She leaned over and kissed him softly on the lips. She put her mouth close to his ear and softly whispered, "I love you, darling. Open your eyes, it's Marnie, please look at me." Brad opened his eyes and looked up at Marnie. She was absolutely elated. He looked right into her eyes. In her heart, she hoped he recognized her, she prayed for it. "I've brought you something so that you'll think of me when I'm gone. She put the earring in his lobe and kissed him softly again. "I'll be back from Florida as soon as I can. I'll call Cally everyday to see how you're doing. Just remember that I love you with all my heart and I'll think about you every minute. I don't want to go to Florida, but I have to because of my Mom." She kissed Brad one more time. Tears streamed down her face. With a heavy heart, she left her precious Brad. She flew to Florida the next morning, thinking that maybe, by some miracle, Brad would regain some of his memory while she was gone, the part that included her.

*   *   *

Carly got up early; she wanted to talk to Chris Jenkins, her attorney. After her coffee and a cigarette, she called Chris. "Good morning, may I please speak with Chris Jenkins? This is Carly Stevenson."

"Hold on one moment Mrs. Stevenson, and I'll see if he's available."

"Thank you." Carly's insides were shaking; she hoped Chris could help her.

"Mrs. Stevenson?"

"Yes?"

"I'll put you right through."

"Carly, how are you? What can I do for you?" Carly explained her dilemma to Chris and he was dumbfounded. "Christ Carly, you've got a big mess on your hands. Well, the first thing you have to do is go right to the head of the hospital and see if he'll give you a copy of the ER admission papers. Better yet, have them mailed to me. That way they'll turn it over faster when they know it's an attorney that wants them. Hospitals hate attorneys. I'll read them and if she signed him in as her husband then we can charge her with fraud. If not, I'll give you her name and you can handle it from there."

"Thanks, Chris. I'll go to the hospital right now and talk to Mr. Stern. I'm sure he won't be happy to see me." Carly hung up the phone feeling determined to get to the bottom of the mystery.

Carly called Cassie and filled her in on what had been going on. She told Cassie that she would call her from Brad's room and tell her what she could find out. As she got dressed, the phone rang; it was the charge nurse. "Mrs. Stevenson, Brad's pretty restless this morning, now that's not uncommon, but I'd like you to come in as soon as possible, maybe you can calm him down. He seems to settle down when you are here."

"I'm on my way now."

Brad was very agitated as Carly entered the room. "Brad, you have to calm down, you can't keep pulling your covers off and thrashing you're left leg around." Carly was worried that he would hurt himself if he didn't settle down. Carly looked to the nurse and asked, "How long has he been like this?

"Since this morning, it's not unusual; reality may be setting in that things aren't right with him. We're hoping that he'll calm down, his barium swallow test is this afternoon and with any luck, he'll be able to eat thickened pudding and sherbet. Maybe that will help."

"That would be wonderful. He's getting so weak and thin. Some solid food might give him the strength and energy that he needs to get better."

There was a knock on the door and the nurse let a man into Brad's room. He looked at Carly and said, "Are you Mrs. Stevenson?"

"Yes?"

"I would like to speak with you out in the hall please, I'm the social worker for the hospital, my name is Eric Watson." Carly followed Eric into the hallway. He turned to Carly and said, "There seems to be some confusion as to who you are. Can you help me clear this up?"

Carly could feel the blood rush to her face; her eyes were blazing. "What do you mean you're confused as to who I am? Brad and I have been married for thirty years; we have two married daughters and three grandchildren. How dare you question me like this! Do you question everyone that's a relative of a patient?"

"Look, Mrs. Stevenson, this is an unusual situation. Brad has evidently told everyone that you and he have been divorced for quite some time now."

"Well, let me set the record straight, we have never been divorced, not now, not ever. And if you don't mind, I'd like you to leave now, and don't come back!"

"I'm so sorry to have upset you, but I have a job to do. Thank you for talking to me and for clearing up the confusion."

Eric left and Carly went back into Brad's room. She closed the door behind her and broke out into tears. How could he have done that to her? Brad had obviously convinced everyone they divorced a long time ago. No wonder they've all looked at her as though she were nuts. Well, one person knew he was married, and that was Marnie. Carly always answered the phone; who did she think she was, the maid? The office knew he was married. Carly's name was on the health coverage, life insurance, their loan, and the car. Either Brad was a great liar, or those people were really stupid. Which ever it was, after she talked to Mr. Stern, there wouldn't be a person left in that hospital that wouldn't know that her and Brad were still married.

If you didn't love me anymore, why didn't you just leave me? Then your precious Marnie would be taking care of you and staring the end of her life in the face, Carly thought to herself as she looked at Brad lying there asleep. It was time to calm down and compose herself, she had to go to Mr. Stern's office and it wouldn't do her any good to be upset. Better to be calm and cool-headed when talking to him.

Brad was waking up and was getting restless. Carly reached over and fixed his pillow. Carly got a cool washcloth so that she could wipe his face. As she was wiping his face, the washcloth got caught on something.

"What the hell is this?" she said aloud. "How dare she come in here and put this thing in his ear, that little bitch! What was she trying to prove? If she loves you so much, why doesn't she come to me like a woman and tell me that she'll take care of you forever? No, instead, she slinks around in the middle of the night or whenever, and leaves little tokens of her love like a thief in the night!"

She hadn't realized how loud she had been talking until Brad woke up. "Please lay back down Brad, I'm sorry. I didn't mean to get you agitated. I know that you don't have a clue as to what's going on and you're not suppose to get upset. Please put your head on the pillow and go back to sleep." Carly took the cool cloth and stroked Brad's forehead until he went back to sleep.

It was time to go head to head with Mr. Stern. Not only do they ask non-stop humiliating questions about her and Brad's relationship, but now she has to put up with midnight visitors to Brad's room. He was confused enough without *her* little impromptu visits. No wonder he's been restless. He was probably upset because he didn't understand those night raids. Stupid little Marnie, she didn't even seem to understand that he didn't even know who he was, let alone anyone else. Maybe she could make Mr. Stern put an end to all of the madness.

Carly walked to Mr. Stern's office, took in a deep breath and opened the door. The receptionist looked up and asked, "May I help you?"

"Is Mr. Stern in? My name is Carly Stevenson and I need to speak with him."

"Just a minute Mrs. Stevenson, I'll let him know that you are here."

Carly pulled her thoughts together as she waited for the receptionist to return.

"Mrs. Stevenson, Mr. Stern will see you now." She opened the door and let Carly into his office.

Mr. Stern extended his hand to Carly and said, "Hello, Mrs. Stevenson, so nice to finally meet you. How may I help you?"

Carly ignored his hand and cut right to the chase. "Look, Mr. Stern, this isn't a social call. I have some serious issues to discuss with you. First of all, let's get one thing straight; I know you are aware of everything that goes on in this hospital. This place in like a small community, everyone knows everyone else's business.

I'm sick and tired of being questioned over and over again about my marital status. Brad and I have been married for thirty years with NO divorce. Whatever anyone assumed is not my concern, the fact remains that I'm being tortured on a daily basis with questions about our relationship and it has to stop. Another thing, the hospital has signs posted with the visiting hours clearly noted. I leave at nine o'clock p.m. to return in the morning to find little gifts. An earring in Brad's ear, to be specific and other small items as well. Don't get me wrong, I don't mind visitors at regular hours, but some of your employees seem to have the need to sneak into Brad's room in the middle of the night. I want this to stop as well.

This person has carried on an affair with my husband for months. I just became aware of this when she brought him into the hospital by ambulance from the motel where they were carrying on. Needless to say I don't want her skulking around the hospital at night leaving little trinkets of love with my husband. She called my home and represented the hospital stating that Brad had to come into work the night of the 29th. She just wanted to make sure he left to meet her. He was so drunk I would have never got him up to go if she wouldn't have called. She said it was an emergency.

And third, the hospital never called me to tell me that Brad had been admitted to the hospital. She called my son-in-law, again representing the hospital, who in turn called me. It's very important that she be told never to set foot in his room again."

"Mrs. Stevenson, I know how upset you must be. I'm very sorry that there was confusion concerning your relationship with Brad, but we were all under the impression that there had been a divorce."

"That's such bullshit," Carly answered back, "you have my name on file for our car loan, life insurance, and health coverage."

"Well Mrs. Stevenson, I can only tell you what Brad told everyone here. And I'm sure that the woman was under the same impression as well. The last thing we want to do is put you under any more stress then you already are. I will make sure no one else questions your relationship to Brad."

"Look, Mr. Stern, I want that woman barred from Brad's room. There's no reason for her to visit him. Christ, he doesn't know who he is, let alone who she is. I've come in his room two days in a row to find him agitated and restless, and I'm sure that it's because she's been in his room at night trying to force him to remember her. I also want her name so that I can deal with her myself."

"Mrs. Stevenson, I can't bar anyone from entering Brad's room. His patient rights would be violated. The only way I can bar anyone is if Brad signs papers stating that he doesn't want her to enter the room."

"Now how the hell can he do that, Mr. Stern? He doesn't know his elbow from his ear; he could never know what he was signing. It looks like you won't give me her name either, so my attorney will be contacting you to get Brad's admission papers. Maybe then I'll get the answers I need."

"Mrs. Stevenson, you do what ever you have to do. In the mean time, I will strongly suggest to our employee that she try not visiting Brad. Frankly, I'm at a loss as to how to handle this situation; nothing like this has ever happened before. I can tell you that the person that you are asking about is out of town for about two weeks due to a family crisis. Please take that time to calm down and concentrate on Brad."

Carly looked at Mr. Stern straight in the eyes and said, "As long as Brad is a patient in this hospital, you and I both have a situation to deal with, and I strongly suggest that you try very hard not to upset me anymore." With that last statement, Carly turned and left, no good-bye, no handshake. As she closed the door behind her, tears streamed down her face. *They're going to stick together, I'm not going to get anywhere talking to anyone here. Chris Jenkins is my only hope.* All this was racing through her mind as she headed back to Brad's room.

CHAPTER TWENTY-THREE

The Climax

Marnie sat in her mother's hospital room in Florida. The weather was beautiful, but her thoughts weren't on the weather, they were on Brad. She had been so busy the first two days taking care of her mother, that this was the first time she could focus solely on him. Her mom's surgery went well, but she had to stay to help with her care. The thought of being away from him any longer then she had to, made her eyes fill with tears. Not being able to be with him was killing her. *What if he needs me? What if he remembers what we had together and I'm not there? He'll think I've deserted him.* She picked up the phone and called Cally. "Cally, hi, it's Marnie. What's going on back there? How's Brad? I'm going crazy down here worrying about him, I miss him so much." Her voice was trembling, and Cally could hear her desperation.

"Marnie, there's not much change in Brad, but you've got bigger problems then him. I checked in on Brad and the earring you put in his ear is gone. More importantly, his wife is all over the hospital trying to find out who you are. It's a good thing that you're in Florida and out of her way. From what I understand, she is very pissed off."

"Christ, Cally, I won't be back for two weeks, what should I do?"

"I suggest you focus on taking care of your Mom and try not to think about Carly. You can't do anything from Florida, so take some time and get a game plan set for when you get back home. I'll call you at your Mom's house tomorrow night."

"Cally, please tell Brad that I love him and that I'll be home as soon as possible. Please promise me you'll see him every day."

"Look Marnie, it's getting pretty sticky around here and as much as I love you, I can't risk losing my job over this. I'll check on him when I can. I'll call you." Cally hung up the phone and thought to herself, *Poor Marnie, she really is kidding herself if she thinks that Brad is ever going to get better and remember her. I told her to find someone that wasn't married, but she wouldn't listen to me. Now all she'll have is memories and a broken heart.*

*   *   *

Carly arrived at Brad's room to find the nurse feeding him sherbet. "Did he have his barium swallow test?" Carly asked the nurse with a surprised tone in her voice.

The nurse looked up smiling and said, "Yes he did, and passed with flying colors. We're starting him out on sherbet and thickened water, and if he doesn't have any problems, we'll upgrade him to creamed foods. As long as he doesn't choke, he should be on a regular soft diet in a few days."

"Then that means he won't need a stomach tube and he'll be off the IV's soon?" Carly couldn't believe what she just heard.

"That's right, Mrs. Stevenson. It looks like this one crisis has passed."

Dr. Collins came into the room with a smile on his face. "This is definitely a step in the right direction. As soon as he gets some of his strength back, we'll move him to the third floor and start his rehab. He'll get speech, physical, and occupational therapy. He still has a long road ahead, but with any luck he'll be able to walk and at least communicate his basic needs. Brad had a massive stroke; most people do not survive one that bad. But he's young and strong, so there's always hope.

He'll never be the way he was, but he shouldn't need a nursing home. He'll never drive again, that's for sure, nor will he ever work. The part of his brain that stores his memory has been severely damaged. What he knows is what he will learn from us and you. At this point, I'm confident that at the least the two years or more prior to the stroke are totally gone and may never come back. It's like teaching a three year old. The other parts of his brain will have to take over for the damaged ones. That can be done, but it will take a lot of work and therapy."

"How long will he have to be in the hospital?"

"Again, with any luck he should be able to go home in about two weeks. His diapers will come off when he gets to the third floor and the heart monitor will be off today. The IV's will stay in for awhile, the antivant for the alcohol and smoking and the heparin for blood thinning and glucose so he doesn't dehydrate. One by one we'll try to take him off of them, but not yet."

Carly thanked Dr. Collins and watched Brad struggle to eat his sherbet. He was so hungry that he tried to eat to fast and choked. The nurse that was feeding him motioned for him to swallow slowly and sit up straight so that he didn't choke again. If he aspirated into his lungs then he could get pneumonia. The inhalation therapist, from then on, would need to come by each day to give a him breathing treatment, to make sure that his lungs stayed clear. After the nurse left, Brad was exhausted and went to sleep. With some food in his stomach, he rested more comfortably so Carly left.

Carly got home and fell into a chair. After the phone calls were made, she had time to digest all the information that the doctors had given her. *He should be going home in about two weeks;* those words echoed though her head. *What if I don't want him to come home? What about my life, will everything from now on revolve around taking care of Brad? What about my job, what about my life? What am I going to do?* She had no answers, only more questions and no one could help her.

After another restless night, Carly headed to the hospital. The one good thing now, was that she didn't have to look over her shoulder since Marnie was out of town. Without that pressure, she could try to sort out her life and what may lie ahead. She reached Brad's room as he arrived back from his MRI test. He was very groggy; they had given him Valium to calm him down for the test. Dr. Matthews came in and gave her the results.

"Well, the test confirmed what we already knew. He had a massive stroke, but he also had many mini strokes prior to that."

"But why didn't I notice something if he had so many little strokes?"

"Well Mrs. Stevenson, the heavy drinking probably masked it, when you or he thought he was passed out from being drunk, he may have been unconscious from a small stroke. Maybe he felt cloudy in his thinking, maybe a little loss of strength, but he could have contributed that also to a hangover. The damage is extensive and it will take a lot of therapy to regain any type of speech or memory."

"Thank you Dr. Matthews, you've given me some significant answers."

As Dr. Matthews left, the phone rang; it was Chris Jenkins. "Carly, I've just received the papers from Mr. Stern. She didn't sign him into the ER as his wife, she signed him in as a "friend," so there's no fraud. But I do have her full name, it's *Marnie Mason*. If you need me for anything else please feel free to call me, you know I'll be glad to help, even if you just need to talk."

"Thanks Chris, you've helped me more then you know." Carly took a deep breath and sat in the chair next to Brad. "Well, I finally have a name. Now, maybe soon, I'll be able to put a face to the name of the woman that you loved so much," Carly told herself aloud as Brad slept.

Several days went by and Brad was moved to the third floor. His days were filled with speech, physical, and occupational therapy. The day-to-day schedule was exhausting for both Brad and Carly. Progress was extremely slow. The therapy now was just to get him well enough so that he could either be sent home or to a rehab center. He was eating a regular soft diet and had gained some of his strength back, but he was still very weak and could only walk with help. The days were hard on Brad, but they were mentally exhausting for Carly. She had to be involved in his therapy. The therapists felt that with her present, he would be calm enough to cooperate. It might have been helping Brad, but it was definitely taking a toll on her.

On one hand, she wanted to help Brad, but on the other, the memories of why she had to help were all too vivid in her mind. Would he be helping her if the circumstances were different? She knew the answer to that already, he wouldn't. He was always too self-centered to have taken time from his schedule to care for her; he would have pawned her off on the girls and went about his merry way. The time was coming when she would have to make a decision about what to do with Brad, take him home . . . or what? There weren't many options.

By the eighteenth day Brad had been in the hospital, Carly's car could drive there on autopilot. Morning, noon, and night all blended together. But something soon would happen to break the monotony, something that she had been waiting for since Brad came to the hospital.

*   *   *

Marnie was finally coming back from Florida. She desperately wanted to see Brad. Cally had kept her informed about Brad's progress and she had hoped that if he saw her he would remember her. Just to look into his eyes and hold his hand after almost two weeks would fill her heart with hope that they would be together again, just like before. She was back on the schedule and hurried into work early to talk to Cally.

*   *   *

Carly stayed later then normal. The hospital was quiet and the nurse suggested that Carly take Brad for a slow walk through the halls. He had to use a cane and the therapist wanted him to practice. Without a lot of people scurrying through the halls, Carly and Brad could take their time without the fear of being bumped. He was still so weak that they couldn't venture far from his room. Even though Brad had lost thirty pounds, he was still a large man, so Carly had to be extra careful that he didn't fall. With her attention focused on Brad, Carly hadn't even noticed the group of nurses that stood at the end of the hallway. As she went closer to the group, she heard a familiar voice. *Where do I know that voice from? I know I've heard that voice before somewhere. Come on Carly, think, whose voice is that?* Just then, Brad stumbled. Carly steadied him and straightened his robe. When she looked up no one was there. *I know I've heard that voice.* All of a sudden it hit her, *That's the voice from the phone call; Oh my God, she's back!*

*   *   *

Marnie almost fainted. "God Cally, I almost ran right into her and Brad. Do you think she saw me?"

"Marnie, that woman was so worried about Brad stumbling; I don't think she saw anything. I hope to God you're going to get over this and get on with your life. It's time to make a clean break and give it up, for your sake and theirs." Cally wanted Marnie to end this craziness, but Marnie was obsessed.

"You don't understand, when he gets better, he'll need me and I want to be there for him. You'll see Cally, we'll be back together just like it was before."

"Marnie, I suggest strongly, that you not go to Brad's room tonight. If she did see you, she might just hang around and wait to see if you come to visit him. Wait until tomorrow night, late, that way you're sure no one will be there with him."

Marnie agreed reluctantly. She didn't want to stay away from Brad, but she didn't want to risk a confrontation, Cally was right. "Just one more day, Brad, I'll see you then."

*   *   *

Carly was haunted by that voice. She called Ann early, before going to the hospital. "She's back Ann, I heard her voice, I know her name, and I know she'll come to see your Dad. What should I do?"

"Well Mom, maybe it's time for you to meet her. Put your cards on the table and see what happens. Evidently, she's not coming to you, so maybe you should go to her. For your sake, it's time to get it over with."

"You're right Ann, it is time."

Carly got to Brad's room before he came back from speech therapy. The social worker left a message that he needed to see her. She left the room wondering what he wanted from her this time. His door was open so she walked in.

"Mrs. Stevenson, nice to see you again."

Carly was not impressed with his pleasant attitude. "You sent for me. What do you need this time?"

He ignored her last statement and said, "Your husband will be released in a few days. We'd like to know what your plan is concerning his discharge."

"What do you mean?"

"Well, Brad seems to fall in a grey area in the system. He's not bad enough to send to a nursing home, we can't keep him here much longer, nor can he go home alone. Unless someone takes the responsibility for his care, we don't know what we'll do with him."

The time had finally come. The time that Carly had dreaded since Brad had come into the hospital. If she walked away, she'd be free. If she agreed to take care of him, she'd be committed, the rest of her life, to be his guardian and caregiver. "How soon do you need an answer from me? Under normal circumstances there wouldn't be any question, but nothing about this is normal and I need time to think."

"I will need your decision by the end of tomorrow. We'll need to make arrangements somehow, if you choose not to take him home."

"You'll have your answer in the morning. I just need some time to think."

"I'll be in my office at nine a.m. Hope to see you then."

Carly shook Eric's hand and left his office. As Carly walked down the hall, she passed the Chapel. She hadn't been very religious lately, but it was as if an arm was guiding her in. As she entered the chapel, Carly's emotions began to overflow. She sat down in a pew and started to cry. *God, why have you put this burden on my shoulders? I was so close to being free, how could you pull me back in like this? I'm not that strong. I don't want to spend the rest of my life taking care of a man who hurt me so deeply. You let him survive the stroke, but in letting him live, you killed me. Not only did they humiliate me; they took my humanity. The thing that makes me a woman is now dead. I have no soul, no heart; I'm hollow inside. What have I ever done in my life to deserve this fate?*

Tears were pouring down her face. All the emotions that she had kept bottled up inside of her for so long now came pouring out. As she looked at the altar, she remembered her wedding day. *For better or worse, in sickness and in health, till death do us part.* All of a sudden, it became so clear. When she married Brad and spoke those vows, she took them seriously. Maybe she had been leaving, maybe she'd had a way out, but now she knew, that was not what fate had in store for her. There was no one else to take care of Brad. His mom wasn't well, and his father was alone and not well either. She could never put the burden onto the girls. *For better or worse. God, I've hardly had the better and if this is the role in life that you want me to play, then you better give me the knowledge and sanity to deal with this. I'm not promising that someday I won't leave, but with your help I'll try my best to do what you want me to do.*

Carly left the hospital and just drove; she needed the night air to clear her mind. Having finally decided to bring Brad home took a large burden off her shoulders and replaced it with a bigger one, but for now, it was the only decision she could live with. Carly drove back to the hospital. It was after visiting hours, but she had to see Brad. He wouldn't understand, of course, but she needed to tell him that he would be going home and that he would be going home with her.

*   *   *

Marnie waited until visiting hours were over. Now she would finally get to see Brad. She could hold him in her arms and tell him how much she loved him. She could hardly keep from running down the hall to his room. Her heart was almost pounding out of her chest; she had missed him so much. Marnie quietly entered Brad's room. She sat down on the bed next to him and kissed him softly on his lips. He opened his eyes and looked at her, "Darling, I told you I'd come back to you. It's Marnie, sweetheart; do you know who I am?"

*   *   *

Carly was anxious to get back to Brad's room. It wasn't that she loved him anymore, but it was time to put their life on the right track. Maybe in time she would learn to live with what had happened and make a life for both of them that was more peaceful and calm. Whatever the future held, she was going to do her best to help Brad recover to his fullest potential. Carly opened Brad's door and she immediately knew who the woman was that was sitting on Brad's bed.

"Well isn't this a touching scene. I thought visiting hours were over, but evidently you create your own visiting schedule."

Marnie's face turned a ghostly white, "Oh my God, I thought you left!" she blurted out.

"Oh, I'm sure you did. I've been waiting for weeks to finally meet the infamous Marnie Mason, and now here we are in the middle of the night, just you, me, and Brad. I have so many things I've been wanting to say to you, yet I don't know where to begin. I've been waiting to meet the woman that my husband couldn't wait to be with day in and day out. Or should I say night in and night out.

Too bad you weren't just a little more patient. I had made up my mind to leave Brad the night before he had his stroke. Just one more day and he would have been all yours. But you had to push for his every spare minute. You were so greedy for all of his spare time that you pushed him over the edge. How long did you think he could keep working and drinking and seeing you? Didn't you see that you were killing him? As for your little nighttime visits, again you only saw what you wanted to see. He doesn't know who he is, let alone who you are."

Carly stepped into the room a little farther, "The last two years of his memory are completely gone, he'll only remember what he's taught, and believe me I'm not going to mention you. The funny part about this, is that he can't remember any of your relationship, but you'll never forget and neither will I. You'll have memories of holding him, kissing him, and sharing his love. Cherish those memories because they're the only ones you'll ever have. Did you think that coming in here, you were going to revive some hidden memory in his mind? Face it, Marnie, he has no memory, and never will. You know; I almost feel sorry for you, but I can't. You see you're going to move on with your life. You'll go to lunch with your friends, work, date, and look forward to a future. Brad is coming home with me. I look forward to wiping drool, changing diapers, and repeating over and over again the simplest of words."

By this time, Carly was standing right in front of Marnie looking into her swollen, tear-filled eyes, "Tell you what, we'll trade. I'll go off and have a life, and you take Brad. But there's one condition; there's no return clause. When you're bored, broke, and old before your time, you have no out, no return. Oh, and by the way, sex; forget about it, it doesn't happen anymore. And since that was such a big part of your relationship, I'll assume your answer to be, no. There are no winners in this situation. You're young; you have a good job. Hold on to the memories you have, you don't want to spend the rest of your life waiting for Brad to have another stroke. I married Brad thirty years ago. I may not love him anymore, but I made a commitment to him and I'm going to try and hold up my end. I'll never forget or forgive Brad for what he did. But I will do my best to take care of him and treat him with dignity. You have seven months to hold in your heart. I also have those same seven months, but I have to try and let them go."

Marnie was sobbing uncontrollably, "How do I move on, I

love him so much?" Marnie's life had crumbled. She finally realized that her dream of Brad ever recovering had come to an end.

"You have two choices," Carly looked at Marnie and in a surprisingly gentle tone, said, "You either take on the full responsibility of taking care of Brad or you walk away forever. You make up your mind. If I don't hear from you before we leave the hospital in two days, then I don't ever want to hear from you again. As far as I'm concerned, you will cease to exist. It will be over."

Marnie got up and ran from the room. Carly covered Brad and fell asleep in the chair. She was too exhausted to go home. In the morning, she would give her decision to Eric.

*   *   *

In the morning, Carly told Eric that Brad would be going home with her. "I'm very pleased with your decision. I wish you all the luck in the world. I know it won't be easy, but I wish you all the best." Carly headed to Brad's room to start packing.

*   *   *

Marnie was packing too. She had decided to go home to Florida; there was nothing left here for her anymore. The new life that had been so promising was over now. It had taken two years to open her heart to someone after her first marriage; it would take even longer to open her heart again, if ever. It would have to heal first, if that was even possible. As much as she loved Brad, she knew that Carly was right. If she took Brad, in a few months she would end up hating the decision she made. Even though she loved Brad, she didn't want to end up resenting him. She'd rather remember the love they had together, than to wish she had never met him. She had written a letter to Brad, hopefully Carly would read it to him someday. She'd mail it to him from Florida, when she stopped crying.

*   *   *

It was time for Brad to go home. Carly arrived at the hospital early. "Brad, its Carly, please listen to me. It's time to leave the hospital. You're coming home with me, do you understand?" Carly's insides were shaking, *What have I taken on? He's scared to death about leaving the hospital.* "Brad do you know where you're going?" Brad shook his head, no. "Look at these pictures; this is where you're going." Carly had brought pictures to help Brad try to remember. "Everyone is waiting for you, Ann, Cassie, and all the neighbors."

You could see the fear in his eyes. The hospital made him feel safe; it was the only home he knew. Carly got Brad dressed, signed his discharge papers, and helped put him in a wheelchair; they were ready to go. Walking down the hall, Carly wondered if Marnie was watching. Hopefully she would start a new life and find happiness—elsewhere.

The outside doors opened to a strange, new world for Brad. He clutched his plastic pitcher and glass like a little child. Friends and co-workers came over to wish Brad all the best of luck. It was time for the new Brad to start his new life.

Marnie watched as Brad left the hospital. She stood behind a large column not wanting to be seen. She knew that she would never see her precious Brad ever again. Tears streamed down her face. She would always love him and she would never forget him.

Brad got into the car and Carly fastened his seatbelt. His eyes were as big as quarters. *Where was he going? Who was he going with?* Carly could feel his fears, "Don't worry, Brad, we'll be home quickly. You'll be fine, everyone will be just fine." *Okay Carly, now it's time to convince yourself. From this point on, your life will never be the same. No more job, no more freedom, and enough responsibility to scare the living hell out of me. Remember God, we have a deal, I'm not promising to succeed, but I'll try if you help.*

A welcome home sign stretched across their front door. Dom and Lindsey, Ken and Mandy were waiting to greet Brad and Carly. Ann and Cassie brought Amber, Cody, and Dakota to see their

Grandfather come home. Yet where was home? Brad had no memory of this place. The only place he knew was the security of the hospital. He felt safe there. This place, home, was not a place he knew, it was unfamiliar and he was afraid. Carly herself was terrified. The man that would walk through their front door was not the same man who had left that fateful night. Once they entered that doorway, they both would embark on a difficult journey. It would be the first day of the rest of their lives.

Amber, at eleven, was well aware of the difference in Brad. Before his stroke, he was a mountain of a man with broad shoulders and muscular arms. His attitude was nasty and he usually dismissed her as an intrusion in his life. Now he was frail and weak. His shoulders were slouched over, and his arms looked like nothing more then twigs off a tree. The confusion of a child of eleven years; how she must have felt at that point was reflected in her eyes; the tears said it all.

Cody and Dakota were far too young to know what was happening. The best part of that scenario was that they would come to know Brad for who he was now, not who he used to be.

Ann and Cassie, on the other hand, had mixed emotions. There was their father, the man who had evoked so much turmoil in their lives; standing in front of them was a man who they barely recognized. How do you separate your emotions? How do you file away years of emotional upheaval and start fresh? Only time would tell how these two young women would deal with their feelings.

Everyone gave Brad a kiss on the cheek, and Carly then asked them all to go home. Brad had had enough for one day and it was time for him to get some rest. It was now time to enter their home. Once the step was made over the threshold, there was no turning back. The absolute terror that filled Carly's heart made her weak in the knees.

The man that stood next to her was the man she married, the man she'd had children with, as well as the man who had hurt her so deeply. But he was not the same man now; this was a man who had lost ninety percent of his brain. Ninety percent of his memory, gone. How do you separate the two? They say that there's a fine line between love and hate. Where did the hate stop and the love begin?

When Brad could think and choose to feel, none of that had included Carly. He was self-centered, egotistical, and cold. Always looking for the next big conquest. Or maybe he was looking for the love he so desperately needed from Jack. When Jack left his son, it left a void in Brad that maybe he kept trying to fill. Even Carly's love didn't and couldn't have filled the emptiness that had consumed Brad's soul.

Brad had had enough excitement for one day. It was time for him to rest. Carly took him up to bed and he started to cry. She could see that he was so frightened, "Oh Brad, I know you don't remember," and the saddest part was, she would never forget.

EPILOGUE

It had been about five years since the stroke, yet for Carly, it had been a lifetime. Marnie had tried to call several times. Carly received a letter in the mail from Florida addressed to Brad with a little red heart as the return address. Carly felt sorry for the girl and for some reason, instead of opening up the letter, she put it in a drawer and threw away the key.

Life had been hard for Cassie and Ann as well the last five years. Cassie was no longer married to Steve. The demons of her past and a need to keep looking for happiness killed her marriage. As hard as she had tried, she seemed to follow in her father's footsteps; always searching for happiness even though it was right under her nose. She got married a second time to a man by the name of Jeff. Hopefully, this marriage would last. For the sake of Cassie, Amber, Cody and her new baby, Angel, she had to try to stop the cycle of pain and let happiness into her life.

Ann and Will were still married, but just barely. Ann had her hands full with Dakota and her new son, Bart. She had to now, battle an alcohol addiction which was slowly consuming her. Cassie always verbalized her feelings towards Brad, but Ann would just make up excuses and cry. The problem with Ann, was that she was a combination of Carly's sensitivity and Brad's wild streak. The battle of the two raged inside of her and the pain she tried to drown almost destroyed her. Hopefully, the scars from her childhood would be able to heal someday and allow her to find peace within herself.

As for Carly, she returned to work part-time, which helped to get her sense of self back. Financially, she had no choice. Jack had helped as long as he could, but she couldn't depend on him forever. As for Brad, he had to get over his fear of not having Carly there every second of every day. Although the job she took was very close to home, just in case, it still gave Carly a brief sense of freedom. For Carly, there was always a mixture of good days with the bad.

Life is not an open book with the story always neatly written. Life is a never-ending set of questions that sometimes have no real answers. Brad had no answers, he didn't even understand the questions. Yet, for Carly, her biggest problem was that there could be no closure.

A PERSONAL MESSAGE FROM THE AUTHOR

I have never been a very religious person. I have gone to church and I have said my prayers, but not on a regular basis. However, through this event in my life, not one day has gone by that I haven't asked God to give me the strength to survive. Our life has gone full circle, it started with love and it has ended with love. I suppose everything else in the middle doesn't really matter. It's been a long journey, hospital trips, illness, and learning to deal with just everyday tasks, but I think when all is said and done, the whole family has become closer and stronger than ever before.

The one thing that my husband has taught me through all of this is to have patience and to laugh. If you don't laugh, you cry and it is a lot easier to have a smile on your face than pain in your heart. It's not the life we planned for ourselves, but many people are going through worse times than what we are. We will still live out our lives with dignity and commitment to one another. The blessing is, *he can't remember* and though there is not as much pain; still, *she can't forget.*